A BLAKE HARTE MYSTERY

UNTOUCHABLE

ROBERT INNES

ISBN: 1540613763
ISBN-13: 978-1540613769

A BLAKE HARTE
MYSTERY
BOOK 1

CHAPTER
ONE

Blake was beginning to think that he had taken a wrong turn. All he could see as he drove slowly round the weaving roads were the same looking trees and bushes with the occasional, equally unhelpful, field. He glanced at the clock on the radio. Half past two. Despite the directions the man on the phone had given him, Blake had found himself driving for a good hour longer than he had been led to believe was necessary.

As he made his way round the next bend, he was forced to slam on the brakes as his car came bumper to bumper with a tractor pulling a large trailer behind it.

Blake looked up at the driver, who stared impassively back at him, then sighed and reversed the car to a passing spot a few yards back. Blake stopped and turned off the engine as the tractor rattled past him, then put his head back against the headrest and sighed. He should have asked the driver for directions whilst he had him trapped.

The clattering of the tractor faded away, leaving Blake sitting in silence. He looked around him, trying to find some sort of landmark that might give him some clue as to where he had ended up. He sighed and checked his phone again. Even if it had any signal, he doubted the maps app would be able to help him with nothing else to type into it apart from 'rather large oak tree.'

Blake glanced up in his mirror and took in his reflection. His brown wavy hair was looking dishevelled and his blue eyes were looking tired. It had been a long morning.

He rolled himself a cigarette and got out of the car. His e-cig was charging, but he rather fancied the more sinful version at this moment anyway. Lighting it, he leant against the car bonnet and looked around him. For about the fifth time in the past hour he inwardly cursed his ex-boyfriend for his current situation, as well as the woman he had discovered him in bed with when he had come home early from work that night. Nathan had been spending a lot of time with her for quite a while but Blake had never even suspected there was anything between them other than friendship – why would he? Nathan was supposed to be gay after all and had appeared to be throughout the entirety of their five year relationship. But apparently the time that Nathan and 'Cassie' had spent in each other's company had lead Nathan to the conclusion that life was 'too short to waste on labels,' and that he 'really needed and wanted to experience these new feelings.'

And so, heartbroken, Blake had walked into the superintendent's office and asked for a transfer. Although he had worked a lot in Manchester, Blake had been stationed at a smaller station on the outskirts of the city– where too many people knew him, knew Nathan and apparently knew Cassie. Superintendent Gresham, his boss for the past seven years, couldn't have looked happier if he had tried when Blake told him he wanted to move.

The two of them had never got on – Blake was a little unconventional in his policing methods. Or rather, he was a little bit too emphatic for Gresham's tastes. He was very much a believer that everybody is driven to the crimes they commit and that nobody is born with the need to perform acts of atrocity. In fact, there were times when he would be working more as a psychologist than a police officer. It wasn't unusual for Blake to spend as much time round a suspect's house, drinking tea with them and trying to understand their motives as it was to see him in the station, doing 'proper policing' and putting people into cells. As much as Gresham had fought behind the scenes, Blake had risen up the ranks to becoming a Detective Sergeant earlier this year, a few days after his thirtieth birthday. Because, as it turned out, his methods got results. It wasn't that Blake couldn't handle the more confrontational aspects of the job – he had been involved in so many raids over the years, armed with tasers and tear gas, that he had lost count and he was never likely to forget the stand offs he had had with people at the height of desperation, armed with some sort of weapon that they were more than prepared to use.

But, despite this, Gresham had never liked him and it was probably this disharmony between them that had led to Blake being transferred here, in the middle of nowhere, as far away from the stuck up prat as possible.

This was getting beyond a joke now though. Yes, he was now to be situated in the countryside, but this was beginning to feel like miles away from civilisation. He half expected to come across a farming shed with the words 'Police Station' written across it in white paint. He hadn't argued when he had been told the location though – he did want to get as far away from Nathan as he possibly could. There was too much deep rooted hurt for him to deal with on a face to face basis. This was his chance to start his life again and to be able to move on from the pain that catching your partner in bed with someone else leaves on a person.

His was just wondering which direction he was going to try next, when his phone started ringing in his pocket, breaking into his thoughts. He pulled it out of his pocket and smiled at the screen.

"Hello Sally-ann." He said, answering it.

He felt his best friend cringe on the other end. She hated being called by her full name.

"You're too far away for me to hit you, but don't think it isn't getting stored away for the next time I see you."

Blake laughed. "If you can find me then that would be worth a slap to be quite honest."

"Why, where are you?"

"Parked between two fields and a big tree." Blake replied, glancing up at it. "Other than that, not a clue. About a five minute drive from the smell of manure? Mind you, you've at least caught me in an area of nowhere that gives me a bar of signal."

"So...lost?"

"Very."

Blake heard her office chair scraping along the floor, meaning she was shuffling along the room to her computer.

"What was the last main road you turned off?"

Blake told her about his movements for the past hour. The time it took for her to find it on Google allowed him to finish his roll up, then he got back in the car, putting the phone on hands-free so that she could direct him as he drove.

Sally was a sergeant in the area that Blake had left behind. Though he had been her superior, they had been such good friends that it had never really affected their relationship. She was an excellent officer and would probably be at his level before very much longer, especially now he was gone. They had shared the same feelings about Gresham and it had been her doorstep Blake had gone to on the night he had found Nathan in bed with that woman. She had helped him find his new house (very much like she was doing now) and had got him horrifically drunk the last time they'd seen each other as a goodbye. If there was one thing he was going to miss more than anything else from his old life, it was Sally-Ann Williams.

Before too long, with Sally's navigation and the luck of him finally coming across a helpful road sign, he was driving slowly through the picturesque market town of Harmschapel – his new home.

It was everything he had expected. A three steeple church, with a plethora of gravestones sticking out of it, a thatched roof pub called "The Dog's Tail" sat on a corner, near a bridge that overlooked a fast running stream and the occasional bus stop. It was a bright sunny afternoon and as Blake meandered along, the sun beams cascaded through the branches of various trees that he passed. Despite the amount of fuel that had been wasted getting here, he had to admit it was a beautiful village.

After a few minutes' drive, he finally found the road he was looking for and turned down it, shortly coming to a stop outside his new house.

It certainly looked cosy. A large wooden door, with two tall hedges either side of it and similar thatched roof to the pub. It was painted white, with two windows sticking out of the top of the building with little tiled roofs on top of them. By the door was a small sign which read "Juniper Cottage." Sally had picked it especially because the rent had not only been within his price range, but because the thought of him living somewhere with the same name as the berry used to make gin had amused her. Although he had loved it from the pictures the landlady had sent, now he was standing looking at it, it looked a little bit less welcoming, almost intimidating – as if it was daring him to mess up now that he had taken these steps and moved away from everything he knew.

He took a deep breath and walked towards the front door, which suddenly opened. A tall woman wearing a silky red dressing gown was standing in the threshold. She had her slightly greying, jet black hair tied in a small beehive on top of her head and looked to be in her early 50s. She smiled warmly at him as he approached.

"Well good afternoon – Mr Harte is it?"

"Yes, that's right. Sorry I'm later than I said I'd be."

The landlady of the cottage moved out of his way so that he could enter. Inside was warm and homely. He was led into the living room, where wooden beams were festooned around the ceiling, various pictures hung on the wall, and an unlit fire sat in the middle of a vast chimney breast.

"Bit of difficulty finding the place then?"

"Yeah, just a bit." He said, scratching his chin. "Sorry, what was your name?"

"Jacqueline." She replied, twirling her necklace round her fingers. "I'm just across the road in the cottage opposite, so anything you need, just let me know."

"Thanks." Blake replied, eyeing the slightly revealing dressing gown she was wearing. "I just want to get settled in to be quite honest. You got the paperwork and everything I sent across to you?"

"Yes, yes." Jacqueline replied chattily. "No problems whatsoever darling." She smiled at him again and leant back against the wall. "A Detective Sergeant living opposite me! I'm sure I'll sleep soundly in bed knowing there's someone of your stature in the village."

She had looked him up and down as she spoke. There was no mistaking it. She was definitely flirting with him. Sally would love this.

"Well, I'll just get out of your way." She said, a little flatly when he didn't reply. "The keys are hanging up on that hook by the door, internet is all connected, heating's on. When do you start at the police station?"

"Tomorrow morning. Is it near?"

"The station? Yes, just round the corner and down the end of the next road." Jacqueline smiled, waving her arms around in an attempt to direct him.

"I'm sure I'll find it."

"Well, Mr Detective, I should hope so!" She laughed loudly and walked towards the door. Blake smiled glibly at her joke and opened the door for her. "Take care, I'll be round tomorrow evening, just to make sure everything's alright and you've settled in nicely."

"See you then." Blake replied.

He closed the door behind her and exhaled. So here he was - the new life. He had only been here five minutes and he already had a middle aged female landlady giving him the eye.

He walked into the next room. The kitchen floor was tiled with stone but the majority of the walls appeared to be made of wood, leading up to the beams in the ceiling. In the centre of the room was a large kitchen table opposite a black electric oven, with a black copper chimney protruding into the ceiling. In the window sill, was a small compact radio that Jaqueline must have left playing. '*Half The World Away*' by Oasis was playing softly out of it. Blake looked around him and shook his head.

"You're not kidding," he muttered.

CHAPTER
TWO

arrison Baxter stood in front of the mirror and lifted up his T-shirt, wincing as he did so. The new bruises glared back at him, dark, purple and standing out fiercely from some of the older, lighter coloured ones. His scalp was burning too from where Daniel had pulled him off his chair on to the ground by his hair.

Harrison sighed and winced again as he pulled his t-shirt up further and turned round. At least the burn mark on the small of his back was going. That had hurt a lot, but he wasn't even sure if Daniel had meant to do it. It was surely easy enough to burn someone with a cigarette and he hadn't even been angry that day.

It was difficult to pinpoint the exact moment that Harrison had realised that he was in, what people called, 'a domestically violent' relationship. At the start, it had all seemed so normal. One day, he had annoyed Daniel to the point where he had shoved him against a wall and shouted in his face. That was no big deal, his own father had done that before. But then, whenever Daniel had gotten angry again, especially if he had been drinking, it would happen again, harder and with more meaning, as if it was an intentional reaction rather than a lashing out. Two years later, his body was covered in various bite marks, bruises and scratches.

As the newest bruises dully throbbed, he remembered happier times. The night they met was at a mutual friend's birthday party. Harrison, then only nineteen, had only just begun to come to terms with his own sexuality, when suddenly he had been introduced to Daniel Donaldson – a confident, funny and above all, gay man in his early twenties. Living on a farm, a twenty minute bus drive away from the main village, had resulted in Harrison leading a rather secluded lifestyle and so to be presented with somebody who was not only like him, but knew how to be like him was nothing short of awe inspiring. The pair had chatted all the way through the night,

Harrison had got drunk and they had ended up sharing a kiss underneath a tree outside the party venue.

After a few dates (hidden from his parents), they had gotten together and Harrison finally managed to pluck up the courage to come out to his parents. His mother had burst into tears and his father had sat in silence for about five minutes then left to go to the pub, not returning till well after Harrison and his mother had gone to bed. After that, the subject was only broached when he needed to know Harrison's location.

A year or so of complete bliss followed however. Daniel and Harrison became inseparable and as the months passed, he ended up spending more time at Daniel's house than he did at the farm.

But, as it happened, the night it all changed, Harrison had been at home. It was three o'clock in the morning when He had received a phone call from Daniel's mother asking whether Daniel was with him. They'd received some tragic news – her husband and Daniel's father had been killed in a car accident.

From that point onwards, things were very different. Daniel began drinking heavily. He was morose, dark and quick to anger. Then that first act of aggression snowballed, quicker than Harrison had realised. But he knew that it wasn't Daniel shouting at him, calling him all the names under the sun, throwing him to the ground and taking all his internal frustrations out on him. It was the drink; it was his dad's death. Once he got through the grieving stage, things would surely go back to the way they were? He, Harrison, just had to be there for him and one day, the Daniel he had fallen in love with would be back. Who was he to say how long someone should grieve the death of their own father?

"Harrison!" His father's voice barking from the bottom of the stairs broke into his thoughts. He gently pulled his t-shirt down again and walked out and onto the landing.

"Yeah?"

"Dinner."

"Coming." Harrison took a deep breath and made his way down the stairs. His parents had no idea about Daniel hitting him – in fact Daniel was always very careful not to hit him anywhere noticeable. All Harrison had to do then was wear clothes that covered up any damaged area of skin. He shuddered to think what would happen if his parents found out. His mother would only be worried. It wasn't worth putting her through that.

He walked into the kitchen, and was immediately gently head-butted by a small bearded goat that was loitering by the open front door. It bleated indignantly as he kneeled down to his level.

"I'll feed you in a bit, Betty." He said soothingly,

scratching the goat underneath the chin. Betty raised her head up to give him access to the spot underneath her beard that she loved having scratched. Harrison had a real fondness for this goat. There were times when he had felt that Betty was his only supportive companion, even if her only displays of affection was when she was hungry.

He gently led her out of the door and closed it behind her, then walked into the kitchen.

His mother, Sandra Baxter was standing over the oven, ladling stew into bowls and his father, Seth Baxter was sat at the table, looking out of the window. He took off his cap and threw it onto the chair as Harrison sat down.

"Bloody hens aren't laying again." He said as Sandra brought him a steaming bowl. "They'll all be in that oven if they don't buck their ideas up."

Sandra sighed as she picked up another bowl and put it in front of Harrison. "Well, Julie's lot stopped laying when they got broody. Give them a few more days before you start talking about putting them in pies or something." She got her own bowl off the counter and sat down.

"Where's the bread?" Seth grumbled.

Sandra tutted to herself and put her spoon down again, before retrieving a bread loaf from the cupboard.

"Did you have a nice time with Daniel, Harrison love?" she asked as she picked a bread knife out of the drawer.

His side throbbed again. Harrison busied himself with prodding his stew about with his spoon. "Erm, yeah. Yeah, it was nice, thanks." He looked up at his mother and it was only then he realised that she was sporting a black and blue bruise around her eye, more distinctive than it would be on a lot of other people because of her pale complexion.

"Mum." He said, frowning. "What did you do to your eye?"

Sandra gave him a furtive look then busied herself with cutting the bread loaf into slices. "Oh, I walked into a door, love. I'd be a danger if I had any brain cells."

Harrison glanced at his father who merely sniffed and said nothing. He had often wondered what kind of son his father had expected to raise and how far away from those expectations reality lay. Being ex-army, Seth was quite strict, standoffish and blunt. He kept most emotions other than anger and indignation very close to his chest. Deep down, Harrison knew that a gay son was not what his father wanted. He had often heard him regaling army stories to anyone who would listen, and none of them brought to mind an environment that Harrison would exactly flourish in.

Sandra brought the plate of bread over and her husband reached across and buttered himself a slice before dunking it in the stew. Harrison felt a lot more uncomfortable over this meal than he normally did. He knew all parents argued but his mother and father did it more than most. But while he had never actually witnessed any violence taking place between them, he knew it went on. He had often heard Sandra let out yelps of pain after the sound of a slap or a thump from downstairs while he was in his bedroom. This was the first time He had ever actually seen her with a bruise though. It seemed both Daniel and his father knew how to hide the results of their outbursts.

A few moments silence followed before Sandra said, "They've got a new Detective Sergeant starting at Harmschapel tomorrow. Julie was telling me."

"Well she'd know." Seth muttered. "Woman's an insatiable gossip."

"She can be," conceded Sandra. "Means well though. She sends her best by the way."

Silence fell again, for longer this time. All that could be heard was the sound of clinking spoons and the occasional squawk from a hen outside the window. Harrison was more than used to these quiet meal times – Seth had never seemed to be big on idle conversation and after working on the farm all day, he often just wanted to sit with his own thoughts, despite the fact that he didn't tend to see a lot of people when he was working.

"I got that final security camera sorted by the way." Seth said finally, chasing a stray carrot round the bowl with his spoon. "Bloody thing wouldn't pick up on the monitor, but I think I've got it working now."

"Oh, that's good," Sandra replied. "Well done."

"Hmm." Seth threw his spoon back into the bowl. "Like to see the little bastards try anything now."

For the past few months, Halfmile Farm had been plagued by looters. They suspected it was a group of lads from further up the hill, who would sneak in and take whatever they could find. The most recent incident had resulted in some of Seth's expensive farming equipment being stolen, so in response he had erected a shed, big enough to hold all of his tools in, the key to which sat on the hook by the living room fire, so that they could keep an eye on it at all times. In addition, security cameras had been placed in strategic areas around the farm so that they could see all angles. Seth had instructed his wife to be as vocal as she pleased about this whenever she was in the village so as to perturb any potential thieves. So far, it seemed to be working. Even so, it was now perfectly normal for him to be in the basement where He had set up the monitors, constantly watching everything that was going on.

Sandra finished her meal and looked up at Harrison. "Grab me down the big washing up bowl from up there will you love?"

Harrison nodded and stood up from the table to reach up to one of the top cupboards where the bowl was located. As he did so, he heard Sandra let out a gasp of horror. "Harrison!"

Harrison froze. In reaching for the bowl, his t-shirt had rode up, displaying the bruises. He quickly pulled it down, but it was too late; Sandra had ran over to him and lifted his top up again. "What in God's name have you been doing? What's happened?"

Harrison glanced at his father who was watching him, eyes wide. His mind whirred, desperately trying to think of a lie. Harrison knew that Seth would do something awful if he found out about Daniel hitting him.

Sandra looked at him expectantly. "Well?" she snapped.

"I was in the village the other night. This group of lads jumped me." Harrison said. Sandra gasped again.

"What? What lads? How many? What night was this?"

Harrison took a hold of her hands. "Mum, I'm fine. I didn't have anything on me, my phone and my wallet were here, so they didn't have anything to take. They just threw me on the ground and kicked me about a bit." His mother went to interrupt him, but he firmly gripped her hands and said "I'm fine."

He glanced across at Seth who seemed to be having difficulty in maintaining eye contact with him. "Are you going to be alright to work tomorrow?"

Harrison nodded. "Yeah. Promise. I'll just go and

feed Betty."

He passed his mother the washing up bowl, smiled reassuringly and then left the kitchen and walked out the front door. As he closed it behind him, he stopped by the window and listened as he heard Sandra telling his father that she thought she ought to call a doctor.

"Leave him alone woman." He heard Seth snap. "He's said he's fine. He's a man, he can look after himself."

The words resonated around Harrison's head. All through his childhood, his father had constantly tried to condition him to be someone who could fight his own battles. He remembered a time when he was about twelve years old and Seth giving him a boxing glove for his birthday. Harrison had half-heartedly punched his father's hand whenever he had been offered it, but he knew that it wasn't enough. Seth would have been happier with a son who wouldn't have any qualms about hitting someone back if they attacked him. Yet, never once had Harrison ever raised a finger to Daniel. He had just closed his eyes and waited for it to be over. Now, he was even protecting him from his own parents. If he had said anything, Sandra would probably have rang the police and Seth would have gone round to Daniel's house and done God only knows what.

As if trying to make him realise something, the newest bruises throbbed again. Two years of lying back and taking the abuse had got him nowhere. All the times he had just assumed his father wasn't proud of him...maybe there was something he could do to change that; maybe it was time to stick up for himself.

He found Betty nuzzling the ground round the side of the house. She bleated at him as he approached.

"Come on then." He said, pulling her across the yard to the old barn outside where they kept her food. As he poured it into the tray she ate out of, his brain continued to whirr. Did he even love Daniel anymore? Harrison had accepted anything Daniel had thrown at him, simply because he assumed that it was a temporary lashing out, but it had continued and continued and continued, until it had reached the point where Harrison was lying to those around him about where he had received his injuries.

He left Betty tucking into her dinner and walked out of the barn back towards the house, his mind made up. Enough was enough. Tomorrow, he was going to end things with Daniel.

CHAPTER
THREE

Blake hadn't slept well. Through a combination of a new bed, the complete silence of the countryside and the worry of starting his new job, when he opened his eyes he felt like he had probably slept for about five minutes.

He clicked his phone to stop the alarm and sat up, immediately whacking his head on the sloping wall above the headboard. He cursed as he rubbed his head, glaring at the offending piece of wall. He glanced around the room where he had dumped his belongings from the car. Suitcases and boxes were scattered everywhere. Fortunately, he had had the hindsight to take out his clothes for the day before he had gone to bed, which were lying on a chair in the corner, though as he looked closer he realised a rather large spider had taken up residency on the crotch of his trousers.

"Good luck mate." He muttered at it, before sloping off into the kitchen.

Twenty minutes later, Blake was showered and walking back into the bedroom with a towel wrapped around his waist. It had taken about five minutes for the shower to be anywhere near the temperature he liked it. His shower back in Sale had a function that remembered what temperature each person living in the house wanted. He had wondered, briefly but bitterly, as the lukewarm water had run weakly down his back what temperature it would have saved for Cassie.

As he looked around his room for his deodorant, there was a knock at the door. He ran down the stairs, still in his bath towel and opened it to find Jacqueline standing there with a warm smile.

"Good morning!" Her eyes wandered down Blake's body, which was still glistening with droplets of water. He moved the door slightly to cover his modesty.

"Jacqueline. What can I do for you?"

She held up a carrier bag. "I just thought I'd make sure you were up and ready for the day. Bought you a few supplies for your cupboard!"

"Oh you didn't have to do..." Blake tried to say but was cut off by Jacqueline pushing past him.

"Oh don't be silly." She beamed. "You go and get yourself dressed. Can't start a new job without a good breakfast inside you! I bet you've barely eaten looking at this kitchen."

She strolled into the kitchen and put the bag on the table and started emptying it. "I know a man and his kitchen. It doesn't stay this clean after you've cooked."

Blake hadn't really felt hungry the night before, in fact he had felt a bit dazed and disorientated by everything. He had been sat in a chair wondering if this was what culture shock felt like.

Now though, he had to admit, he was ravenous and watching Jacqueline take out bacon and eggs wasn't helping. A big breakfast probably would make him feel better, although he did wonder if Jacqueline was doing it for her own reasons rather than to actually help him.

By the time he had come downstairs again, Jacqueline had already buttered him some toast to be getting on with and started frying bacon in a huge frying pan that had been hanging over the cooker.

She looked up as he re-entered the kitchen. "Oh, very smart!" She said approvingly. "It's been a while since I've cooked for a man." She smiled, though Blake could detect a hint of sadness in her eyes.

"And who was that?" he asked, sitting down.

"My husband." She replied, filling the kettle up. "He died…five years ago it'll be now."

"I'm sorry."

"Oh." She waved a hand in what Blake assumed was an attempt to appear careless. "These things happen. He was a good man. He had the unhealthiest lifestyle though." She began haphazardly cracking eggs against the side of another pan and dropping them into it. "Never touched fruit or vegetables unless I force fed him them. Mixed in with a thirty a day smoking habit and a dodgy heart, he was a bit of a ticking time bomb. I came downstairs one morning to find him face down in a bowl of cornflakes. Still though," she turned to him and smiled, a hint of flirtation in her eyes. "Life goes on."

Blake gave her a slightly grimaced smile. He didn't feel that it was quite the right time to mention his sexuality, especially when she had gone to all this effort.

"Yes." He said slowly. "Well, you'll find yourself someone if that's what you're looking for. Who can resist a good cook?"

The compliment seemed to satisfy her for now and she dished up the breakfast she had made for him.

When he had finished, he glanced at the clock on the wall. "Well Jacqueline, that was amazing. Thank you so much. I really need to be going now though."

"Oh absolutely, yes. Mustn't be late on your first day. " She stood up from the table and passed him his coat. "Good luck, Detective. I hope it's an easy first day for you."

Blake took his coat off her. "Yeah," he murmured. "So do I."

Blake arrived at the station fifteen minutes early. It was a lot smaller than the one back in the city. Two police cars sat outside it. Other than that, there didn't appear to be a lot of movement. It was a far cry from the bustling hive of activity he had come from where the sound of sirens constantly filled the air and officers were forever running out of the doors.

He walked inside it and down the corridor towards the reception desk. To his surprise, there was just one woman sat on her own behind the glass. There was nobody else around and she seemed to be doing what looked like a crossword puzzle.

Blake cleared his throat as he approached. The woman, portly, mid-fifties with her greying hair tied back, glanced up at him.

"Yes?" She said dryly.

Blake eyed the crossword puzzle and where her pen was hovering over it. "Four down is '*despondent.*'"

"I'm sorry?"

"Four down. The amount of little ink dots that are

on it suggest you've been trying to work that one out for a while. '*In low spirits, no hope,*' ten letters. '*Despondent.*"

She looked down at the page and glared briefly at him before filling in the answer. "Thank you."

"You're welcome."

"So, have you come in just to give me a hand on my crossword or can I help you with something?"

"Well, I hope so. Detective Sergeant Blake Harte. I'm starting here today."

The crossword quickly vanished.

"Right, yes." The woman said, standing up. "I'll just take you through to the briefing room."

"Thank you." Blake said coolly. "What was your name?"

"Darnwood. Mandy Darnwood." He raised his eyebrows expectantly. "Sir."

He simply nodded, making a mental note that he was going to have to keep an eye on this particular officer.

She took him down another corridor where he could begin to hear a group of people talking and laughing. As he entered the room, the noise stopped. The six or so occupants turned to look at him as if he had just entered a western saloon.

Darnwood cleared her throat and called across the room to the office at the other side. Inside was a man in his late fifties, "Sir, this is D.S Harte."

The man looked up from his desk and stood up. He was quite tall but rotund with a distinguished and bushy moustache. "Ah, yes!" He exclaimed, standing up and walking towards them. "Hello!"

Blake guessed by the way that he was dressed that this was to be his new boss. He liked him more than Gresham already.

"Inspector Royale." The man said, shaking Blake's hand. "Welcome aboard. Found the place alright then?"

"Sir." Replied Blake. He had never understood why anyone asked that question to people standing right in front of them.

"Well, let me introduce you to the team." Royale beamed. "Sergeant Mandy Darnwood, you've already met."

Darnwood twitched her mouth in what Blake assumed was an attempt at a courteous smile and walked out of the room.

"Everyone, bit of quiet." Royale instructed, even though nobody had said a word since Blake had walked in.

"This is our new Detective Sergeant – Blake…?"

"Harte." Blake replied.

"Yes, yes. Detective Sergeant Harte. Soon to be Inspector from what I'm told." Royale paused impressively. "D.S Blake is formally from Manchester C.I.D, so a little bit different here from what you're used to I expect." He chuckled and then gestured to a man with a neatly trimmed moustache sitting behind one of the desks. "Over there is Sergeant Gardiner."

Gardiner glanced up from his computer, an air of distinct moodiness about him. "Hello."

Blake was slightly bemused as to why a man who looked to be in his late forties appeared to be quite so surly.

"This is P.C Patil," Royale continued, indicating a young Indian woman sat closest to them. "She's a fairly new recruit herself, so I'm sure you can teach one another a thing or two."

Patil stood up and held her hand to shake Blake's. "Hello, sir." She said genuinely. "Nice to meet you." Blake shook the much friendlier hand.

"Oh and this is our youngest recruit!" Royale chuckled as a man who couldn't have been any older than about twenty- one entered the room carrying a tray with steaming mugs on.

The young officer looked up, slightly terrified at the new arrival. "Oh," he said, placing the tray down on a desk. "Hi. I'm Billy. Mattison. Sorry, P.C Mattison." He stood up straight in what Blake assumed was his way of trying to look professional. Blake appreciated it, nevertheless.

"There's a few others, but you'll meet them in time, I'm sure." Royale said.

The sound of a phone ringing came from the

corridor. Blake wondered if Darnwood would put down her crossword to answer it.

"Well, you get yourself settled in, D.S Harte." Royale beamed. "You'll soon learn how we do things around here."

"Sir!"

Darnwood walked into the room, clutching a piece of paper in her hand. "Just had a call for a car to go up to Halfmile Farm. Reports of a disturbance? Something to do with Daniel Donaldson."

"Donaldson!" Gardiner exclaimed, jumping up from his seat. "Got the little sod."

"Daniel Donaldson?" inquired Blake.

"He's a repeat offender sir." Patil replied. "Not that we've been able to nail him down for anything, other than the odd drunken fight outside the pub."

"He gave me a nosebleed once." Mattison muttered. "I'd love to see him sent down."

Blake nodded. "I know the sort. Let me guess, council house, seven hundred kids and a girlfriend who sits at home and does what she's told?"

Gardiner scoffed. "He'd have a job with that." He put his hand up then bent his wrist delicately. "He's like that. Right, let's go."

Gardiner's words resonated around Blake's head. He strongly suspected that Sergeant Gardiner and he were not going to get on.

"Well, why don't you go too?" Royale said as

Gardiner, Patil and Mattison hurried out of the room. "Give you a sense of location and all that."

Blake nodded and hurried out of the room. Outside, he met the other officers by one of the cars and climbed into the front.

"You coming with us, Sir?" Mattison said, looking slightly excited.

"Yep." Blake replied. He could already tell that Mattison was keen to impress.

Gardiner rolled his eyes at Mattison and climbed into the driver's seat. He started the engine and they sped off towards Halfmile farm.

CHAPTER
FOUR

T hat morning, Harrison had woken up early. The sunrise sent beams of gentle light through the gap in his curtains. He had sent a text to Daniel asking him to come to the farm when he woke up the previous night. Despite being quite a heavy drinker, Daniel had always been an early riser, so Harrison was expecting him to arrive within the next couple of hours.

The familiar clattering of buckets and closing metal gates told him that his father was already up, and at work. Harrison's only job that day was to clean out the chicken sheds, but he didn't need to do that till later that afternoon.

He stood up and went to the window to open the curtains. Seth was walking towards the shed where all the equipment was stored. Harrison watched him unlock it and place a few tools inside before remerging a few moments later, slamming the door behind him. He locked the door and walked briskly across the yard.

Harrison went downstairs to the kitchen where his mother was already halfway through her morning clean of the house.

"Morning love." She said, looking up. "Sit yourself down, I'll get you a tea. It's just brewed."

Harrison sat down at the table, phone in his hand. He was waiting for the text from Daniel that said that he was on his way. It normally took him about twenty minutes to walk down from the top of the hill to the farm.

Harrison had been rehearsing all night as to how he was going to do this and what he was going to say. He had gone from almost suggesting they have a break until Daniel had sorted himself out, to wanting to completely end it. The lying to his parents about the bruises had gone some way to making him realise how absurd the whole thing was. He had been there for Daniel through the toughest period of his life, only to have it, quite literally, shoved back in his face.

Sandra placed a large steaming mug of tea in front of him and hovered over him for a moment. Harrison glanced up at her. Her black eye shone proudly back at him. "You alright, Mum?"

She hesitated, then sat down next to him. "How are those bruises doing sweetheart?"

Harrison nodded. "They're alright. I can barely feel them."

"Well, that's because you're a tough lad," she leaned in confidentially. "No matter what your dad says."

Harrison smiled back at her. There was a pause, then she placed her hand over his and stared at him with an intense look of concern in her eyes.

"Whilst your dad's not here, do you want to tell me where they really came from?"

Harrison froze. "What do you mean? I told you, I got..."

"Harrison Baxter," His mother replied, kindly but firmly. "You had that exact same expression on your face when you were twelve and I asked you if you knew who had smashed that big vase in the living room.

Harrison looked down at the floor, apparently telling Sandra all she needed to know. "Oh, love..." She murmured. "How long has this been going on for?"

Harrison looked up at her, his brain lamely attempting to formulate an excuse, but failing. Instead, he just sighed. "A couple of years."

"Harrison." She groaned, talking a grip of his hand. "I had a feeling. I knew something like this was going on. Just the way you were around him. You know you need to end it with him, don't you? If he's hitting you, that's it.

He raised an eyebrow at her. "You're one to talk."

"Look, never mind about me. I'm alright. But listen to what I'm telling you. Use me as proof if you like. It's only going to get worse. Can you honestly do this for the rest of your life?"

Harrison nodded. "He's coming over in a bit."

His phone suddenly pinged as a text message came through. It was from Daniel. 'On way,' was all it said.

"Coming over *now* in fact." Harrison said nervously. "I'm ending it today. I'd already decided."

Sandra squeezed his hand reassuringly. "Do you want me to be nearby?"

Harrison shook his head. "Just give us some space would you Mum? I need to do this on my own. And for God's sake, whatever you do, don't tell Dad. He'd go mad if he knew, you know that."

Sandra had a strange expression on her face, as if she had never been more proud of him than at that moment. She nodded. "I'll make myself scarce, but you shout me, as loud as you like, if things get a bit…"

"I will. Don't worry, I'll be fine."

Sandra leant over and hugged him. "Good luck son." She said, before disappearing out of the front door.

Twenty minutes later, Harrison was stood in the kitchen, watching Daniel turn the corner on his way down the hill towards the farm. This was it. His heart was hammering in his chest at the thought of how Daniel was going to react to what he had to say and now he could see him walking towards him, he had completely forgotten how he had been planning to word it.

Daniel arrived at the front door and walked in without knocking. "Alright?" he said. Harrison looked at him standing in the doorway and a feeling of dread ran through him. He was drunk.

"Dan," Harrison began nervously. "I need to talk to you."

Daniel stumbled forwards and put his arms around Harrison, gripping him tightly. The smell of stale beer hung off him. "What's wrong?" he slurred.

Harrison attempted to pull back from him but Daniel held his grip. "Dan, let go," He gasped. "Please."

Daniel loosened his hold on Harrison and stared at him. "What's wrong with you?" He said, a touch of accusation in his voice. "Aren't I allowed to hug you?"

Harrison looked up at him nervously.

"Well?" Daniel snapped. "If you've got something to say, *say it*. Dragging me here this early, what –"

"It's about us." Blurted Harrison. "I'm sorry, but I

can't."

"You can't what?"

Harrison took a deep breath. "I can't do this anymore. I'm sorry. Please don't go mad." There was a long silence. Harrison's heart was thumping wildly. Daniel's eyes were wide. "What? Why? What's wrong with you? What are you on about?"

"I can't be this person anymore, Dan." Harrison lifted up his t-shirt to reveal the bruises on his side. "This isn't what you do to someone you love. I've tried waiting, I've kept quiet, I've lied to people about why I'm covered in bruises and I can't do it anymore!" Now he had started, the words were flowing out like a stream. "I'm walking around in pain Dan, most days! Every single time I take my clothes off to have a shower or something, all I can see and feel is where you've hit me, where you've kicked me and I *can't* do it anymore."

"But you said, in fact you admitted that the other night was your fault. You said '*I'm sorry Dan, I messed up*,' those were your exact words!"

"All I'd done was try to tell you to stop drinking Dan." Harrison replied, trying to sound as forceful as he could. And all you did was pull me to the ground by my hair and kick me on the floor – because *that* is what you get like when you're drunk! Sometimes not even then, when you're sober. I mean, look at you!

40

You're drunk now! Have you even been to bed?"

"Don't you judge me. You know what I've had to deal with and you said you were there for me, you *promised* me you'd support me!"

Daniel's voice was raising and he stepped forwards menacingly. Harrison stood his ground. "Supporting you is one thing, but just letting you lash out at me whenever it gets too much for you isn't what I'm here for. None of this is my fault, so why are you treating me like it is? I didn't kill your dad, did I?"

The words had escaped before he could stop himself. Daniel stared at him, his face contorted in anger.

"I'm sorry, I didn't mean to word it like that –"

But before he could say anything else, Daniel had grabbed him by the throat and pushed him against the wall. "Is this a *joke* to you?" He shouted. "My Dad dies and it affects me, turns me into a screw up and you think you can just drop me because *you've ran out of ways to help*?"

"Dan-"choked Harrison as his grip tightened.

"You are not going anywhere." Daniel growled, his face inches from Harrison's. "Say it. Say you're not ending this, *tell me you're lying*!"

Harrison couldn't have said anything even if he had wanted to, Daniel's fingers were too tight round his throat. Suddenly, everything happened at once. There was another voice shouting in the room and

Harrison had been thrown back to the ground, gasping for air. His vision was blurry through the tears in his eyes as he looked up to see Seth standing over Daniel who looked like he had be launched across the room and had landed against the table.

Seth's eyes were wide with fury. "You are *done* here." He growled. "How do you like it, eh? Being bullied?" He picked Daniel up by the scruff of his neck and frogmarched him out of the kitchen.

Harrison stood up and ran after them. "Dad! What are you doing?!"

Seth was striding with the struggling Daniel across the yard and towards the tool shed. His hostage stumbled and fell to the ground, but was quickly hauled up and forced towards the door of the shed.

"Harrison, go and get me a phone." Seth snapped. He pulled the key to the shed out of his pocket and opened the door. "I'm calling the police and THIS PIECE OF DIRT isn't going anywhere till they arrive!"

He threw Daniel into the shed and slammed the door, holding the door closed with his hand.

"*Oi!*" roared Daniel from inside the shed. "*Let me out!*"

Daniel's foot kicked heavily against the door as Seth placed his shoulder against it to stop him from escaping.

"This is the end of you bullying my son! By the

time I'm finished with you, you'll be rotting in a cell."

He pushed the key into the lock and turned it. There was another bang against the door. Seth turned round to Harrison and walked towards him. "Come on. He can't get out now."

Harrison stared at the shed and then ran after his father back into the house.

"Where's the phone?" Seth snapped as he strode into the kitchen.

Harrison wordlessly pointed to his mobile on the table. His father picked it up and pressed the screen. "Well, unlock the bloody thing then." He thrust the phone back into Harrison's shaking hands.

Harrison stared at the shed. He hadn't wanted Daniel to be arrested for what he had done to him, it hadn't even occurred to him. "Dad, do we have to do this?"

Seth didn't say another word, he merely clicked his fingers loudly and held his hand out for the phone. Reluctantly, Harrison gave it to him.

Seth furiously dialled and put the phone to his ear before storming out of the kitchen. Harrison watched him leave, then took a deep breath to try and calm himself down. He looked at the shed. There was no way he was going to be able to get Daniel out of there now, Seth had the only key.

Harrison walked back out into the yard and towards the shed. He could hear his father asking for police on the phone. How had it come to this from that one kiss underneath a tree?

As he approached the shed, there was another, quieter thud against the door from inside.

"I'm sorry Dan," Harrison called, softly. "He's calling the police. They'll be here soon." His brain whirred, trying to think of something supportive to say. "Just know that I didn't want any of this to happen."

He walked round the shed, desperately attempting to formulate a plan. "You'll get the help you need, Dan. I promise. You won't get sent down or anything, I'll make sure of it. They'll talk to me, it'll be fine. I promise."

"Harrison!" shouted Seth from across the yard. "Get away from there, stay away from him!"

Harrison glanced at the shed again and walked back towards his father. "Dad," he murmured imploringly, "If you let him out now, he'll go. I've ended things with him, he won't be back."

"You say that now." Grunted Seth. "But he'll worm his way back into your life. This way, he can't do that. The police will make sure of it. Now, wait inside."

"But Dad –"

"Wait inside Harrison." He replied firmly. "I won't tell you again."

Harrison sighed and walked back into the kitchen.

There wasn't any point in arguing and he didn't have the fight in him to stand up to both of them.

He sat at the table and put his head in his hands trying to think about what he was going to say to the police. He had no experience in anything like this – maybe if he really pushed how much the death of Daniel's dad had affected him then they'd surely have to have some sympathy with him then? There would be something he could say or do to make the situation better. He took another deep breath. It would be fine. Everything was going to be okay.

CHAPTER
FIVE

Blake glanced up the road as the farm started to come into view.

"Why do they call it Halfmile farm?" he asked.

Mattison poked his head out from the back seat. "Because it's half a mile up the hill, Sir."

Blake bit his tongue. The countryside was starting to get on his nerves now.

Throughout the whole journey, Gardiner didn't say a word. Patil and Mattison were in the back chatting and Blake was fairly sure he could detect a bit of a spark between them. He remembered when he had been a police constable and there had been a bit of a romance between two of his colleagues of the same rank. It appeared some things were to remain the same.

"So, where did you say you were from, Sir?" Patil asked him.

"Well, I was stationed in Sale just outside Manchester." Blake replied.

"How come you moved from there? It's probably loads busier than here, isn't it?" Mattison said.

"I just fancied a change, that's all." He answered simply.

"In a massive city like Manchester though, imagine." Patil gave a small chuckle. "I bet you had gangs and murders and drug dealers and all sorts to deal with there."

"Well yeah. It certainly had its moments." Blake conceded.

Gardiner scoffed as he parked the car at the entrance to the farm. He then got out and slammed the door sharply behind him.

"What's his problem?" Blake inquired as he undid his   seatbelt.
Mattison glanced at Patil. "Well Sir, I think the position you've filled by coming here is the one he was after. Sergeant Gardiner has been after a promotion for years."

"And if you hadn't have arrived, he'd probably

have got it, Sir." Patil grinned.

"Oh I see." Blake nodded as he climbed out the car. He could imagine how irksome Gardiner would find it to be after a higher position for so long and then to find himself stuck where he was when a younger upstart like himself came in and trod on his toes.

Blake looked around him. The farm seemed to be of a pretty good size with the house right in the centre of all the action, but looking up, Blake was surprised to see a security camera staring back at him from the top of one of the fences. Glancing around, he realised there were quite a few all pointing to different areas of the yard and beyond.

"Is this sort of security normal round this area?" he said to Mattison, indicating the cameras.

"Oh, yeah." Mattison replied, looking up at the camera. "They've had no end of thefts and break-ins round here. The man who lives here, Seth Baxter, he stuck up all these cameras and put up that shed thing over there to keep all his stuff in."

Blake was just about to start walking towards the house when he was suddenly pushed forcefully from behind, sending him flying forwards and landing on a heap on the ground. He spun over looking for a culprit but instead found himself eye to eye with a small angry looking goat.

A young man came out of the house and ran

towards them. He was young looking, blonde and had a body that looked fairly muscular underneath his t-shirt. He also looked very nervous.

"Oh my God, are you OK?" He panted, pulling the goat away from Blake. "Sorry about Betty. She's just trying to be friendly."

"Friendly?" repeated Blake, picking himself off the ground and rubbing his knees. "I'd hate to see her when she doesn't like someone."

"Hello Harrison," Mattison said. "You alright? We've had a call saying there's been a disturbance?"

The young lad nodded. "Yeah, that would have been my Dad?"

"And where's your Dad?" Blake said, narrowing his eyes as he spotted a small red bruise on Harrison's neck.

"I'm here." A man in his late fifties was striding across the yard towards them from the house.

"And you're the one that called?"

"That's right. I've got Daniel Donaldson locked up in that shed."

"Well done, Seth." Grinned Gardiner. "What's he done?"

"Hang on a minute," Blake cut in. "Locked up? Why have you locked him up?"

Seth looked Blake up and down. "You're the new man I suppose?"

Blake looked at him, surprised. "I have just moved

here, yes. Why?"

"Because if you'd been here a while, you'd probably know that Daniel Donaldson is the type that needs locking up." Replied Seth curtly. "Harrison, show them your bruises."

"I can see a bruise on your neck there, Harrison." Blake said, ignoring Seth completely. "Has Daniel done that to you?"

Harrison glanced at his father nervously and then nodded.

"And the rest," Seth snapped, pulling Harrison's top up. Blake recoiled. Harrison's lower body was covered in an array of bruises and marks.

"This is what that boy has done to my son." Growled Seth, loosening his grip on Harrison's T-shirt. "Answer your question does it? Now, like I said, he's in that shed. So if you can just-"

Suddenly, the sound of a gun firing echoed around the yard. Blake quickly turned around, as everyone ducked down on the ground.

"What the hell was that?" Gardiner exclaimed, who had thrown himself behind the police car.

Blake's eyes darted around the yard. "Who owns a gun in this area?"

"I do." Replied Seth, cautiously standing up. "It's kept in that shed, where I've locked him up."

Blake looked over at the shed. Since the gunshot, everything had gone deathly quiet. Even the animals around the yard had fallen silent.

"Then you better get it open, hadn't you?" Blake murmured.

They all walked across the yard towards the shed. Seth pulled the large key out of his pocket, then turned back to Blake.

"He's an aggressive little yob. I hope you know how to handle people like that."

"I've done pretty well so far." Blake replied.

Seth unlocked the shed door and opened it, stumbling backwards as he pulled the door open. They all stared in amazement as a body of a man fell out of the threshold and onto the ground.

Blake quickly turned the body over and felt for a pulse.

"Dan!" Harrison cried.

Blake frowned as he tried to find some form of life around the man's neck. No pulse. He looked up at Harrison.

"This is your boyfriend?"

Harrison nodded, eyes wide with horror.

"Shall I call an ambulance, sir?" Mattison asked, pulling his radio towards his mouth.

Blake sighed and nodded. He then stood up and pulled Mattison away from the others. "Though I don't think an ambulance is going to do him much good to be honest."

Mattison stared at the body on the ground. "You

mean he's dead?" He whispered.

Blake sighed again. "Yeah. I think he is."

Mattison took a deep breath. "Right." He had gone quite pale and looked shaken. Blake recognised that look.

"Is this your first one?"

Mattison nodded.

"OK. Well, pull it together, yeah?" Blake said, not unkindly.

"Yeah. Yeah, of course."

"Good lad. Right, so yes. Call an ambulance but I'd get forensics down here as well. I'm obviously not in a position where I can declare him dead. They'll have to call it officially."

Mattison nodded again and walked away, talking into his radio. Blake was certain that there was nothing any paramedics could do at this point. Daniel had that glazed expression on his face that Blake had seen several times before.

Harrison was stood staring down at Daniel clearly choking back tears and ran his hands through his hair. "He's dead isn't he?

Blake walked back towards them. "I don't know. An ambulance is on the way."

"But how?" Harrison cried. "I don't understand how this has happened!"

Blake kneeled down and looked at Daniel closely. He had a small wound, probably from a bullet across the side of his neck, a second in his chest and another one lower down near his abdomen.

"Seth, you're saying that you locked him in here?"

Seth nodded. "Yes! I threw him in, locked the door and then went to call you." He looked in the shed, an expression of confusion across his face.

"So, where is this gun, Seth?"

"Think he shot himself? Couldn't take the guilt anymore? It's in a locked case in there."

"Is it loaded?"

"Of course not. And yes, before you ask, I have a licence for it."

"Well, we'll obviously be checking that." Blake replied curtly. "And it's always locked in here, separate from the bullets?"

"Yes. Of course." Seth snapped.

Blake frowned. "You always lock this shed when you aren't using it?"

"Always." Seth replied, looking very confused. "Every single time without fail. I'm the only one with the key! Nobody could have got in!"

"Well if that's the case," Blake murmured, kneeling down beside Daniel's body again. "Then nobody could have got out either. And when you locked Daniel inside this shed, there was nothing wrong with him? He was fine?"

"Of course he was!" snapped Seth. "What do you take me for? I threw him in here, then locked it. He couldn't have got out. And nobody could have got in."

"Then what the hell has happened to him?" Gardiner interjected from behind Harrison.

"How long ago did you call the police?" Blake asked, ignoring Gardiner.

"About twenty minutes ago or so."

"And there's only you two here?"

"Seth!"

The sound of a woman's voice rang across the yard. They all turned to see a woman in her late forties running towards them.

"What's going on?" She panted. She looked down at Daniel's body and gasped. "Oh my…Seth! What's happened?!"

"Sorry, what's your name?" Blake asked her.

"This is my wife, Sandra." Seth replied, putting his hand on the shoulder of the scared looking woman.

"I heard a gunshot!" Sandra exclaimed. "What's happened? Is Daniel alright?"

Harrison was stood, staring at Daniel with a horrified expression on his face.

"Sandra," Blake said, taking Harrison by the arm. "Where were you when you heard the gun shot?"

"She was feeding the animals." Seth interrupted.

Blake glared at him. "I'm sure your wife can talk for herself, Seth." He then talked over Seth's objectionable grunting. "Whereabouts were you?"

"Erm, just round the corner there." Sandra

murmured, pointing to behind the house.

"Right. Patil, I need you to take Sandra and Harrison inside."

"Come on Sandra. Nice cup of tea, that's what we need I think." Patil said soothingly.

Harrison had started to cry. Sandra put an arm around him and walked him back into the house with Patil. Seth watched them leave, his lips thinning. Blake wondered if he was trying not to cry himself. As he watched Harrison go back into the kitchen, he spotted one of the security cameras, which was trained directly on the shed.

"Seth." Blake said. "Will you be able to show me what that camera has recorded over the past hour?"

Seth seemed unable to speak for a moment. "Hm? Oh. Yes, certainly."

"Sir?" Mattison was walking back towards them from across the other side of the yard. "They're on their way."

"OK, thanks." Blake said. "Right. Mattison, with me. Gardiner?"

Gardiner looked up from the body and up at his new boss with a slight twinge of annoyance, presumably at being addressed by his surname. "I need you to stay here with Daniel and the area needs securing."

"Me?" Gardiner looked furious at such a suggestion. "Why me?"

Blake stood up straight and with authority. "Because this man has been shot in a room that nobody could have got in or out of. Right now, the only way that seems possible is if he did it himself and, judging by the way his wounds are positioned, I don't think that's what happened. I need someone to stay with him and wait for the ambulance. Is that alright or do you need me to explain myself further?"

Gardiner looked like he wanted nothing more than to punch Blake on the nose. Blake glanced up to the end of the yard. A group of lads on bikes had spotted the police car and were trying to see what was going on with interest. "First thing you can do is get rid of them." Blake said finally.

Gardiner didn't say another word. He just stormed off towards the group of lads.

"Thanks!" Blake called after him with a tone of sarcastic cheeriness. He turned to a smirking Mattison who quickly wiped his expression clean. Blake gave him a brief grin then indicated that he should follow him.

A few minutes later, Blake was sat in front of the monitor in the basement, trying to find the right camera for Seth to rewind.

"Right then." He muttered. "Take that one back about an hour…"

Seth clicked the mouse so that the footage sped backwards. "Right, around there, would you say?"

The film returned to normal speed and for a few seconds all they were looking at was still footage of the shed. The angle allowed them full sight of the door and the left hand side of the structure.

"Can you speed it up a little bit?" Seth reached for the mouse, but Blake took it in his own hand and clicked it so that the footage went forward faster, ignoring the disapproving tut behind his head.

A minute or so went by with nothing happening on the screen until Seth came into view. Blake clicked it so that it went back to real time and studied the screen.

"This was about half an hour or so before it happened." Seth said. "Look, I'm carrying the hose that I was using to wash out the pig sty. The gun is kept locked up behind where I keep the hose, and the case hadn't been interfered with, I distinctly remember seeing it."

Blake kept watching, now without fast forwarding. He wanted to see everything that had been happening around the shed before Daniel was put into it. As it turned out, very little *had* happened.

Suddenly, Seth and Daniel appeared on the screen, Seth had his hand on the back of Daniel's neck and was frogmarching him towards the shed. There was no mistaking, Daniel was definitely alive when he was being pushed inside. They continued to watch as Seth unlocked the door and, as had been reported, threw him inside, slamming the door closed again and locking it.

He then stormed back towards the house, but not before turning round and shouting something at the shed.

"What did you say to him then?" Blake said, pointing towards the screen.

Seth shrugged. "Something about him not being able to get away doing that to my son."

Mattison spoke up from behind Blake. "What exactly was he doing to Harrison when you walked into the kitchen?"

Seth sighed. "He had my son pinned up against a wall by his throat. He was shouting, hurling abuse. Absolute lowlife. I picked him up and threw him against the kitchen table. Then, I took him towards the shed and put him in it, like you've just seen."

"And nothing else happened between you pulling him off Harrison and you walking him towards the shed?" Mattison asked.

"No, nothing."

Blake rewound the footage a few seconds and watched again as Daniel was put into the shed and locked in. He then let it play on.

A few moments later, Harrison came into view.

"What's Harrison doing?" Blake asked, to nobody in particular.

They watched as Harrison walked towards the

shed and stopped outside it. He then wandered around the right hand side and out of view of the camera.

"Oh, he'd wandered up there, feeling all sorry for him." Seth grumbled. "I shouted to him to leave it alone and he came straight back towards the kitchen." Seth replied.

"So what did he do whilst he was round here?" Blake murmured. He tapped the side of the shed on the screen where Harrison had gone out of view of the camera's sights.

"Well, very little I would imagine." Seth said reproachfully. "I hope you're not trying to accuse my son of anything?"

"Sir?" Patil appeared at the basement doorway. "The ambulance is here."

"OK," replied Blake. "Can you take Seth to talk to them please? We'll be up shortly."

Seth didn't look like he was very keen on the idea of leaving Blake and Mattison on their own with his cameras but Blake wasn't really leaving him with a lot of choice. Reluctantly, he followed Patil up the stairs.

"Oh, one more thing Seth?" Blake called. "Why does your wife have a black eye?"

Seth stared at Blake levelly. "She walked into a door."

Blake nodded curtly, then indicated that Seth could leave. Once he had gone, Blake continued watching the footage. Once Harrison had apparently been called by his father to come away from the shed and had walked back towards the house, there was very little else going on aside from the odd chicken foraging for food around the shed.

"Right then Mattison." He said quietly once Seth had left the room. "Actually, what do you prefer to be called?"

"My friend's call me Matti." The young officer replied, looking pleased that he was already on such familiar terms with his new officer in charge.

"Alright then Matti…What do you think?"

Mattison looked flattered that his opinion had been asked for.

"Well," He shrugged. "I think it's impossible for a man to be locked in a shed alive and then to be dead when the door is opened again. But that sounds stupid, I know. Sorry."

"Don't apologise," Blake said reassuringly, not taking his eyes off the lack of action on the screen. "You're right. It isn't possible. So that means that something else happened to Daniel Donaldson to result in his death."

A few minutes more passed by as they both watched the footage in silence. Nothing else happened until Blake saw himself come onto the screen as they all walked towards the shed. The door was opened and Daniel's body landed on the ground in front of them.

"Did you say he couldn't have done it himself?"

Mattison asked as Blake paused the footage.

"I don't think so." He replied, shaking his head. "He had one wound across his neck, one here," He pointed to his chest, "and then another one down here." He gestured towards his own stomach area. "I've seen people's bodies after they've committed suicide from shooting themselves. One bullet, that's all it takes because that's all you can get out of a gun yourself once you've pulled the trigger. You don't shoot yourself more than once just to make sure."

"And you think he's definitely dead?"

Blake nodded grimly. "I was sure from the moment he fell out of the shed to be honest. I just didn't want to say in front of Harrison."

He leant back in the chair, thoughtfully. "There's one more thing that doesn't make any sense here and I think you can work out what it was. Aside from someone apparently managing to be invisible and walk through a solid wooden wall of a shed and back out again. Think back to when we heard the gunshot."

Mattison frowned. After a moment, he raised his eyebrows in surprise. "We only heard it once."

Blake grinned at him. "Exactly. One gunshot doesn't equal three separate wounds on a body."

"So that means the gunshot we heard had absolutely nothing to do with it?"

"Maybe, maybe not. But I think we were certainly meant to think it was Donaldson being shot. Come on." He stood up from the chair and walked back upstairs. "Time to talk to the boyfriend without his father standing over him I think.

Blake and Mattison walked back upstairs to the kitchen, where they found Harrison sat with his mother, his head in his hands, Patil sat opposite them.

Sandra looked up at the two of them as they entered the room, looking concerned that they were going to upset him further.

"Harrison?" Blake ventured gently.

"He's still very shaken." Sandra said quietly.

"I can understand that. But I'm going to need to talk to you so I can find out as much as I can about Daniel." Blake knelt down to Harrison's level and put a supportive hand on his shoulder.

Harrison looked up at Blake, his eyes red and puffy.

"I didn't…" he uttered, shakily. "I didn't want anything like this to happen."

"Of course you didn't. I know that." Harrison looked up at Sandra. "Could you give us some space?"

"Oh, but he's in no fit state to -"

"I still need to talk to him now. Whilst it's fresh in his brain. Sooner I've done this, the sooner it's over. That alright, Harrison?"

Harrison took a deep breath to calm himself and nodded. "It's fine Mum." He said, wiping his eyes. "I'll be alright."

"Thanks Sandra." Blake said, turning to Mattison and Patil. "Can you two take Sandra outside, I don't want anyone else coming in."

"Yes, Sir." Mattison put up a gentle arm to lead Sandra out of the kitchen. She reluctantly allowed herself to be taken outside and Mattison shut the kitchen door, leaving Blake and Harrison alone together at the kitchen table. Blake saw one of the paramedics standing outside. "I'll just be a second Harrison." He said.

The paramedic looked up as Blake greeted him by the door.

"Good morning. I'm DS Blake Harte."

"The man in charge?" The paramedic said.

Blake nodded.

"Well then you've got more work to do here than we have I'm afraid."

Blake sighed. "So, he's dead?"

"'Fraid so."

"Ok, thanks."

As the paramedic walked back towards the ambulance, Blake saw a forensics van pull up on the driveway. He hoped he could at least trust Gardiner to explain everything to them whilst he spoke to Harrison.

CHAPTER
SIX

Harrison was rather struck by this new policeman sat in front of him. Through the explosion of horror, confusion and upset of the past hour, Harrison had seen a level of humanity in this man that he hadn't really sensed in anyone before.

His father was an emotionless husk at the best of times, his mother merely flittering around like a moth against a light bulb trying to keep the day as easy and positive as she could and then of course there was Daniel, the reason he was covered in bruises, who was now lying dead in his front yard. But as Harrison looked up at the understanding and kind face in front of him, he felt that he wasn't going to be judged, whatever answer he gave. Bizarrely, despite everything that had happened, he was almost feeling relaxed now it was just the two of them together.

"What did you say your name was?" Harrison asked, timidly.

"DS Harte. You can call me Blake if you want to though."

"Blake Harte. Nice name."

"Thank you." Blake replied. There was a pause. "Harrison, I've just spoken to the paramedic. I'm sorry but there's nothing they could do for Daniel."

Harrison wasn't shocked but the confirmation caused him to put his head in his hands again as the realisation flooded though him.

"Do you want a drink?" Blake asked him.

Harrison took a deep breath, then nodded. "I'll do it." He said, standing up. This man might be a detective but he would challenge Sherlock Holmes himself to find anything in this kitchen after one of his mother's epic tidying sessions. He flicked the kettle on then leant against the counter, taking another deep breath.

"So." Blake said, putting his hands together. "Are you OK to do this now?"

"Yeah. I think so."

"When did you and Daniel first meet?"

"About three years ago." Harrison replied. He could see a group of people in white jump suits around the shed. His mother and father were with the other two policemen watching proceedings. "I was going to break it off with him today actually. Well, I did I guess. That's why he went mad at me."

"Is that where the bruises on your neck came from?"

Harrison instinctively put his hands up to cover the marks, then realised that there wasn't any point now. Maybe that was why Daniel had grabbed him like that, because there wasn't going to be anything to hide from anymore.

"Yeah. He had me pinned up against that wall shouting in my face. He was drunk, as he normally was."

"How often did he hit you?"

Harrison thought for a moment as the kettle boiled. "I don't know really. Often enough. I remember the first time seemed like a lashing out. But then it happened again. And again."

He poured some hot water into a mug, then realised he had forgotten to put a tea bag into it. "Sorry, I forgot to ask, did you want one?"

"I'm fine." Blake replied. "Did he ever do anything else to you? Other than hitting?"

Harrison got a teabag from the top cupboard and put it in the mug, stirring it in with a spoon. "Erm, well yeah. He called me names a lot. That only tended to happen when he was really drunk. I don't know why but the name calling hurt more. He'd get really personal. Telling me that I was a coward and a wuss. Loads of things."

"You can't have been that much of a coward if you broke it off with him today?" Blake offered. "Was that all it ever was? Just hitting you and name calling?"

"What else is there?"

Blake hesitated. "Did things ever get a little bit scary in the bedroom?"

Harrison's eyes widened. "What do you mean?"

"Did he ever want to have sex when you weren't in the mood?"

Harrison glanced up through the window at his parents. They were a safe enough distance away for him to talk.

"Well, yeah. Sometimes we'd be in bed after he'd hit me or something, feeling me up and stuff. I kind of just let him do it, I didn't want to make him angry again. If he was in that sort of mood, you know, touching and stuff, then that meant that he wasn't angry anymore. So I'd just let him do it."

Harrison was surprised to see a flash of sadness cross Blake's face but he quickly seemed to pull himself together.

"So, today – you've told Daniel you want to end things, and he, like you say, '*goes mad?*'"

Harrison took a sip of his tea and sat down at the table again. "Yeah."

"Then your dad comes in?"

"Yeah."

"What happened then?"

"I'm not sure really." Harrison said, taking another sip of his tea. His neck still felt a bit tender. It felt bizarre to be feeling physical pain from somebody who was now dead. "It's all a bit of a blur. I looked up and Dad had Dan on the table. He looked like he was about to punch him. Then he sort of picked him up and took him outside."

"Towards the shed?"

Harrison nodded.

"And you followed?"

"Yeah. I didn't know what Dad was going to do. I've never seen him that angry."

"Does your Dad get angry very often?"

Harrison faltered. Did he really have to know that?

"Harrison?"

"Erm, sometimes. Not as often as he used to, nowhere near."

"What did he used to do?"

Harrison looked at him imploringly. "Do we have to talk about that?"

"I'm just trying to paint a picture, Harrison. That's all." Replied Blake kindly. "But yeah. I'm sorry, but I do need to know."

Harrison took another large mouthful of tea to try and waste a bit more time. "He used to. He's smacked me before, you know, when I was younger."

"So your Dad has been violent to you?"

"Yeah, but not for ages!" Harrison said quickly. "I mean, years. When I was a teenager probably."

"Has he ever hit your mum?"

"No."

"Are you sure? I noticed your mum has a black eye?"

"Yes." Harrison replied. He didn't really see what any of this had to do with Daniel's death. There was a pause, then Blake thankfully decided to move on.

"OK. So, back to this morning." Blake continued. "Your Dad takes Daniel outside, opens the shed and then locks him inside it. Where were you at this point?"

"I was standing just by the kitchen door."

"So, you could see everything that happened?"

Harrison nodded. "Dan was banging up against the other side of the door, trying to get out. Dad locked the door and came back towards the house, telling me to pass him my phone so that he could call you. He went outside to ring you and then I went to try and talk to Dan."

"You did. I saw on the cameras. You went up to the shed walked round the side. What were you saying?"

Harrison smiled sadly. "I think I apologised. Can you believe it? Everything he'd done and I was the one saying sorry."

"Did he say anything back?"

Harrison shook his head. "Then my Dad called me back inside." He sighed, the emotion of the morning's events flying back through him. "I can't believe this has happened. I did love him you know. I know that sounds stupid. I'm stupid. I must be to put up with all of it for that long." He started crying again.

"Hey." Blake said, putting a supportive hand on his arm. "None of this is your fault. Domestic violence is one of the hardest things to get out of. And you did it. You got out of it. He died a single man. That isn't stupid. That's brave. I admire you."

"Really?" Harrison looked up at Blake, immediately wishing he wasn't crying. He certainly didn't feel particularly brave at that moment.

"Really." Blake smiled. "And some day, you're going to find a bloke that treats you how you deserve to be treated and they're going to be lucky to have you."

There was a moment's silence as Harrison calmed himself down and gave Blake a small smile.

A knock on the kitchen door interrupted them. The policeman Blake had come up from the basement with poked his head round the door.

"Sorry Sir but you're going to want to see this. We

think we've found the gun."

"OK, Matti. Thanks. I'll be out in a sec." He turned back to Harrison and pulled out his mobile. "Look, I haven't been here five minutes yet so I haven't got a card or anything for the station or a number you can get me on there. So, for now, just take my number. If you think of anything else, anything at all about what happened, then give me a call or a text. OK?"

He scribbled his number down on a notepad that was on the side of the table. "I think I'm probably going to have some more questions for you at some point. But you've been really helpful for now. Try and calm yourself down, alright?"

And with that, he stood up and strode out of the kitchen into the yard. Harrison looked down at the number on the pad and the name written underneath it. Blake Harte. Despite everything that had happened, Harrison already felt just a little bit happier.

CHAPTER
SEVEN

Blake strolled across the yard towards Mattison and Gardiner. He absolutely hated dealing with domestic violence victims, and it seemed to him there was more of it going on around Halfmile farm than the victim and his ex-boyfriend. He already got a vibe from Seth Baxter that suggested somebody who would be quick to fly off the handle and his wife's black eye along with the age old excuse of 'walking into a door' only fuelled his suspicions.

"So where did we find this?" Blake inquired, eyeing up the weapon. It was a shot gun.

"We found it at the other end of the yard, behind the shed." Gardiner said shortly, clearly still annoyed at being given such menial tasks to perform.

The woman from forensics pulled her facemask down. She had brown hair and brilliant blue eyes. "This has been fired recently. But having looked at the victim even for a minute, this gun wouldn't create the types of wound on his body. A gun like this tends to make much more of a mess, there'd be gun powder residue and the wounds would be bigger. I can say with some degree of certainty that this isn't your murder weapon.

"Really? Have you got any gloves?"

She passed him a pair of latex gloves out of her bag.

"What was your name by the way?" Blake asked as he pulled them on.

"Sharon. Sharon Donahue."

"Nice to meet you Sharon. DS Blake Harte. So, why was this fired?" He said, examining the gun.

"There's other officers with the Baxters' now, Sir." Patil announced, as she walked towards them.

"Excellent. They're separated, yes?"

"Yeah."

"Right then," Blake said, passing the gun back to Sharon. "With your permission Sharon, I'd like us to take a look at that shed."

Daniel's body had now been removed, which

meant that Blake was going to have to wait for the post mortem results from the coroner. It was already one of the strangest murder investigations he had ever come across.

"I don't suppose there's any chance that there could have already been somebody in there waiting for him, is there?" Mattison asked as they arrived at the shed.

"Don't be stupid." Gardiner snapped. "We were all out here when the door was opened, we'd have seen if anybody else was in there."

"I don't think there's anything stupid about it." Blake said sternly. "I'm yet to hear any helpful suggestions from you, Gardiner?"

Gardiner glared at Blake. "Suicide. It must have been. If nobody else was in there and the boy's been shot, then it must have been suicide."

"No chance." Sharon said. "The way the bullet wounds are placed, there's no way he did it himself. We're going to have to get him examined before we can say anything for certain."

"Now that was stupid." Mattison grinned.

"You just behave yourself Matti." Chuckled Blake. Gardiner didn't say a word, he just seethed with his arms crossed like a petulant child.

"We're going to have to get someone to inform his family." Blake said as he opened the shed and examined the door. "Somebody sensitive, obviously."

"Do you want me to go, Sir?" Patil asked him.

"Well, are you sensitive?" Blake inquired jokingly. He found it easier to create a lighter atmosphere with his officers during cases like this. They had a serious job to do, but if things were too heavy then the mood amongst colleagues had a tendency to be more counterproductive.

Gardiner scoffed. "She's going to have to be more than sensitive to get through to Donaldson's mum."

Blake turned round to give him a withering look. "And why is that?"

"Because she's an alcoholic. The whole family is a mess. Mini will probably be trying to tell an unconscious pile on the floor that her son's dead. She probably doesn't even remember she has a son right now. Her daughter's in prison as well by the way, for grievous bodily harm"

"When did his sister get sent to prison?"

"Two months ago. I was the one who made the arrest," Gardiner added, a tad smugly. Blake wasn't impressed. "She broke into the corner shop in the village but didn't realise that the owner was still out the back doing a stock take. He surprised her and she beat two rounds of crap out of him. I don't know what she was after. Money, vodka or cigarettes probably."

"If you think you can tell his mother Patil, then yeah. I'm happy for you to do it."

"Sir." Patil said, walking away towards one of the

cars.

Blake entered the shed. It was longer than it was wide meaning that the only way it was possible for more than one person to stand inside was in front of one another rather than side to side. All around the walls was expensive looking farming and gardening equipment; a strimmer, large secateurs, hoes and a long rake positioned delicately in a diagonal direction across the wall. An orange lawnmower sat at the back, and just by the door was the hose he had watched Seth place back inside here on the camera. A large metal case was sat behind it, its lid ajar.

"Sharon, pass me that gun a second." He said.

She passed him the shotgun and he placed it inside the case. It certainly fit inside it the way he imagined it was supposed to. So why was it out of its case? Who had fired it and why had it been found on the other side of the yard?

Looking around, he quickly saw that there was absolutely no way anybody was going to be able to get in or out of here, apart from the door that he had come in from.

"Right, so Harrison came out of camera view, around here." He murmured to nobody in particular as he came out of the shed and round the side, looking up at the camera pointing at the shed until he could see that he was out of its sights. He looked at the wooden panels in front of him and pushed against it.

"Right lads, give it a kicking. See if any of the panels are loose."

Mattison and Gardiner went to work on the wall of the shed pushing and kicking each of the large wooden planks. It soon became clear that none of them were moving. Neither did any round the back of the shed either. It seemed the whole structure was completely impenetrable, as something built to protect anything from potential thieves was supposed to be.

"What about the roof?" Sharon suggested.

Blake shook his head. "We could see the whole roof from the security camera. Nobody or anything was up here."

He pulled his e-cig out of his pocket and sucked thoughtfully on it.

"It must have been Harrison." Gardiner put in. "He's the only one with any motive. How many times do you see it? Battered partner, sick to the back teeth of having the stuffing kicked out of them, finally loses it and kills the abuser."

"So how did he do it?" Blake asked him impatiently. "Where did he get a gun from?"

"Look, I don't know how he managed to shoot him through a solid wooden wall, but it's obvious it's him. You saw him, he's a wreck."

"Because his boyfriend has just been murdered!"

"Yes, and he's the one that did it! Mattison told me, on that CCTV camera, he comes towards the shed and comes out of view. He's the only person who came near enough to do anything without being seen."

Blake sucked on his e-cig irritably. He trusted his own instincts and he couldn't bring himself to the conclusion that Harrison was responsible, but unfortunately Gardiner had chosen now to finally start talking some sense. Logically, from what he had seen on the camera, Harrison was the only person who could possibly have done it but, as far as Blake was concerned, that was purely circumstantial at this point. After all, logic hardly came into a situation where someone had been murdered in such a baffling way.

CHAPTER
EIGHT

That evening, they made their way back to the police station. As the afternoon had drawn on, Blake and Gardiner's relationship had become ever more fraught. Gardiner's insistence that Harrison was the culprit for Daniel Donaldson's murder grew and grew despite the fact that he couldn't produce a single piece of solid evidence to support his theory. The problem was that Blake couldn't produce any to counter his argument with either, aside from the fact that Harrison, to him, just didn't seem capable.

By the time they'd driven back to the police

station, in close confinement with each other, a heated discussion had developed into a full blown argument.

Blake stormed into the station, slamming the door to the conference room open as he entered with Gardiner in furious pursuit.

" So, like I've asked you, at least a *hundred times*, give me one, *just one*, good reason we can charge *anybody* for Donaldson's death at this stage?!" Blake shouted, leaning against one of the desks and glaring at Gardiner.

"Because he's the one –*the only one*– who could have done it!" Gardiner roared back, a muscle bulging slightly at the side of his head.

"Did you interview him?"

"What does that have to do –"

"*Did* you interview him?"

"No!"

"Then please, for the love of *God* tell me how you think you've got anything that puts him in the frame!"

"Because it's the only thing that makes sense *Detective!* What, you think just because he's bent that he doesn't have it in him?" Gardiner spat, slamming a folder from his desk back onto the shelf.

Blake stormed across the room using the journey from the desk to Gardiner to calm himself down enough not to do anything other than shout.

He stopped a few inches away from him and pointed at him, furiously. "Two things. If you ever and

I mean *ever* use that sort of homophobic language in front of me again, in fact even when I'm not here because I'm very good and I will know, then I swear to God I will personally see to it that your policing career goes no further than you putting out the odd traffic cone. *And number two!*" He shouted over Gardiner's attempts to interrupt him, "Number two, I am your superior officer and you *will* talk to me with respect, even if you don't agree with me. Do I make myself clear?

There was a small cough behind him. "And what is going on here?"

Blake spun round to see Inspector Royale standing in the doorway to his office. Blake hadn't seen him when he had stormed his way in in such a rage. He wasn't quite sure how to respond.

"Michael, I think it's probably home time for you now, don't you?" Royale said calmly to Gardiner.

Gardiner grabbed his jacket from the chair in front of him and threw one last furious glare at Blake. "Sir." He snapped before marching out of the room.

"And you Billy. Long day for all of you. Go home and get some sleep."

Blake hadn't noticed Mattison even follow them into the station. He was stood awkwardly in the doorway to the conference room, having been shoved aside by Gardiner as he had left.

"Yes, Sir." Mattison replied politely.

Blake watched as Mattison left the room and walked down the corridor.

"A word, DS Harte?" Royale asked just as calmly. He stood aside so that Blake could enter his office.

Blake closed his eyes in dread as he walked into the room. He couldn't believe he was in trouble with the new boss on his first day. Gresham would kill himself laughing if he could see this.

"Well, what a first day you've had." Royale said as he closed the door. "Do sit down."

Blake sat, watching Royale make his way around the desk. "Tricky case. It's been some time since we've even had a murder in Harmschapel, never mind one that sounds so utterly beguiling."

"I'm sure we'll make some progress pretty quickly." Blake reasoned.

"Oh I'm sure." Royale smiled, sitting down opposite him. "But in the meantime, might I suggest you dispense with the old '*I'm your superior*' routine?"

Blake sighed. "Sir, Gardiner has an attitude."

"He's slightly set in his ways, I grant you."

"It's more than that Sir. Gardiner is just a –"

"Yes?" Royale said, eyebrows raised.

Blake swallowed the insult he was about to utter, then briefly paused whilst he thought of something slightly less abusive to say. "An annoyance." was the politest he could manage.

Royale leaned back in his chair. "In what way?"

"In the way that his attitude absolutely stinks, Sir. He's rude, he's arrogant, he's got no respect, he makes homophobic comments and he -"

"And," finished Royale. "He thinks that somebody you believe to be innocent is responsible for this murder this morning. If it's as illogical as it's been described to me, you can hardly blame the man for having precious few other theories."

"I understand that Sir, but -"

"I would ask you to give Michael a bit of slack." Interrupted Royale. "He's in the process of going through a very bitter and difficult divorce at the moment."

"I see."

"As well as that," Royale continued. "And you may not be aware of this, but he was rather hoping to occupy the position that you filled when you transferred here."

"That was mentioned to me, yes." Blake conceded.

"I accepted you instead of him because of the recommendations I was given about you from the Superintendent and that has rather put Michael's nose out of joint. I would hate to regret that decision because of a lack of, shall we say, adaptability on your part?"

Royale stood up and made his way towards the door. "Blake, I know you to be an excellent detective. I understand that you've got a slightly more unorthodox way of doing things and I actively encourage that as I would anything that has been proven to get results, such as your career has. However, I would ask you to remember that you aren't in the middle of a bustling city squad anymore." He opened the door and held it open. "This is a quiet, countryside town. I understand what these city boys are like, you need to keep order and control. But that isn't needed here. I don't want you to fall foul of any accusations of unprofessionalism or, dare one say it, bullying. Am I clear?"

Blake realised there was very little point in arguing. "Sir." He conceded quietly.

When he got home, Blake slammed the door behind him and threw himself into the same chair he had occupied last night. He had been planning on doing all of his unpacking when he had arrived back but he was too agitated and annoyed to even think about doing that now.

He leant back, took a deep breath in and exhaled slowly. There was a moment of calmness that was immediately shattered by a knock at the door.

Resisting the urge to scream at whoever it was to leave him alone at the top of his lungs, he groaned and reluctantly went to open it.

"Post!" trilled Jacqueline.

"I don't want any." Blake replied shortly. But he opened the door further and walked back into the lounge so that she could follow him in.

"Oh dear!" Jacqueline said, closing the door behind him. "How was your first day?"

"Not the best."

"No." Jacqueline replied. "I heard about the death at Halfmile farm."

Blake looked at her, bewildered. "How?"

"Oh." Jacqueline waved her hand dismissively. "Word gets around in a small village, you know how it is. Especially something like this – Is it true? That he was locked in a shed then somehow shot whilst he was still inside it? It's like something from one of my crime novels!"

Blake sighed. "It's only early in the investigations."

"Well," Jacqueline said enthusiastically. "Me and the girls were throwing a few ideas around, you know the way you do."

A feeling of complete exasperation flooded through Blake. "You were doing what?"

He then remembered the group of lads leaning over the far fence at the farm from a distance watching proceedings that he had sent Gardiner to get rid of, which was presumably how word had travelled so fast.

Jacqueline threw down the letter she had been carrying and produced a large sheet of A4 out of her pocket and flattened it out on the table.

"So, if he was in the shed." she began. "Then there

was absolutely no way he could have got out, only here where the door is." She said, pointing to a small cross that she had already put on the paper.

"Jacqueline, I can't discuss this with you." Blake tried to interrupt her, but she continued regardless, pointing at different areas on the diagram enthusiastically.

"Which means that it happened inside the shed, had to have done. So what if there was some sort of remote control device? You know the sort of thing you can get in this day and age, it's scary – anything is possible. Something that would have shot him when he was in the shed and would have been activated by that wireless thingee. Oh, what's it called? *Wi-Fi!* All they have to do is make sure that he's in the shed and then press a button or activate it, and boom!"

She looked up at Blake wide eyed, waiting for his reaction. Despite how irritated he was by the interruption, Blake was quite touched by how much effort she had put into the diagram which was really rather detailed.

"Thank you," He said gently. "But, like I say, I cannot discuss this or any case with you. It's confidential."

Jacqueline looked extremely disappointed. "Ah well." She said, folding the diagram up. "Rules are rules I suppose."

"But, I'll certainly consider what you've said as a

form of investigation." Blake promised, lying through his teeth.

Jacqueline nodded dejectedly and put the diagram back in her pocket.

"I tell you what, leave that. Do you mind? That could really help me actually." Blake said, holding his hand out for the diagram.

That did the trick. Jacqueline appeared delighted. "Oh! Well, yes of course!" She handed it back to him. "Anything to help! Well, I'll let you get back to it then. Oh, that letter arrived for you by the way. I got chatting to the postman and he left it with me when you were out, sorry."

"That's alright. See you later."

When he had finally gotten rid of her, he let out another sigh, then glanced at the diagram. How the hell had Donaldson been shot? As much thought as Jacqueline had put into her explanation, Blake could quickly discount it. The idea of a remote control device wasn't necessarily a bad one, but how could anyone have got into the shed to set up such a device when the Baxters' were the only one with a key? There was a vague possibility somebody could have stolen it but there had to be easier ways to shoot the man.

He walked across to the table and picked up the letter she had left behind. Expecting it to be junk mail or a bill, he carelessly ripped it open but was surprised when he found what looked like an invitation made of card inside. It was from his ex, Nathan, inviting him to the *'happy and forever'* wedding of him and *'the beautiful Cassandra.'*

It was the perfect end to the perfect day. He stared at it in furious disbelief for a few moments before tearing it up and throwing the pieces across the room. That did it. He needed a drink.

CHAPTER
NINE

Harrison walked through the street, his eyes stinging from all the crying he had done that day. That had to have been one of the worst rows he had ever had with his father. He was still trembling.

It had started when Harrison had innocently asked Seth who could have been responsible for shooting Daniel – it did, to him, seem a pretty reasonable question seeing as though it had happened so bizarrely and also in their front yard.

His father had been on edge all evening, understandably after the day's events, so Harrison hadn't really reacted when he had had his head bitten off when Seth had snapped, "How the hell should I know?"

Both of his parents had spent most of the day being questioned by the police, although Blake had only spoken to him. In fact Harrison was concerned about the fact that the man in charge had been the one talking to him and not any of the lower ranked officers. Did that mean they thought he did it?

The stress of the day had resulted in the argument going from a simple exchange of words to a full blown row. Seth had screamed at Harrison, criticising his choices, his lifestyle and his general demeanour when it came to standing up for himself, the finale of the vitriol being that if Harrison had just been *'normal,'* then none of this would ever have happened.

Harrison had shot back that the only thing he had ever wanted was to make his father proud and had been told that that was unlikely to ever happen.

It had gone on and on until two officers that were stationed at the farm had had to intervene to calm the situation. Harrison had stormed out of the house and down the hill into the village, tense and anxious. His father could be terrifying when angry and tonight had been no different.

As he walked through the village, he felt everyone's eyes on him. He hoped he was only imagining the murmured whisperings around him – did they all think he had done it too?

Harrison wasn't a huge drinker but before too long he found himself striding towards The Dog's Tail pub. A few people were stood outside smoking, quickly falling silent as he approached. One of them, a woman he vaguely recognised from the post office, gave him a polite nod of acknowledgment as he pushed past them inside the pub then went into a frenzied whisper with the two friends she was with.

When he walked inside, he was relieved to see that it was fairly empty, apart from a huddled group of people in the corner who glanced up at him as he entered and then resumed their conversation.

"Hello, Harrison." Robin, the landlord of the pub was standing behind the bar, wiping a glass and looking sternly at him. "What can I do for you?"

"Erm, just a pint please."

"You sure that's a good idea, all things considered?"

"I just want one pint."

A voice rang out from the other side of the room. "Thinking about what you've done over a drink?"

Harrison turned to see where the voice had come from and his heart sank. It was Craig Samuels, one of Daniel's best friends although Harrison had never felt especially welcome to share Daniel's friendship with him. He was wearing a red tracksuit, a gold chain around his neck that barely covered the tattoo on his neck and a cap that nearly shielded his eyes.

"Craig."

Craig stood up, kicking his chair aside.

"How did you do it Harrison? Daniel was my friend, one of my best friends – don't you think I have a right to know how he died?"

Harrison backed away slightly. "Look, I don't know how it happened – I swear."

"You're a liar." Craig snarled, walking towards Harrison. "He gets shot at your house – who else would it be? Tell me how you did it."

"I didn't do it!"

"I don't believe you."

"Ok, that's enough." Robin the landlord said sharply. "Harrison, I think it would probably be better if you left."

"Yeah, that's a good idea." Craig smirked. "Why don't we all leave together?"

"No, I don't think much to that idea as it happens." Harrison turned in surprise at the new voice. Blake Harte was standing right behind him, glaring at Craig.

Craig gave him a disdainful look. "And who are you?"

Blake pulled his wallet out of his pocket and opened it to reveal his identification. "Detective Sergeant Blake Harte. I'm new round here so I don't think you and me have had the pleasure? Mr...?"

Craig scoffed. "I don't have to tell you my name."

"No, not yet you don't." Blake replied casually. "But I get the feeling me and you are likely to meet again, under far more professional circumstances. Until then?"

Craig gave a last glare at Harrison then turned to his crew at the table. "Come on."

They all downed their pints and stood up, aggressively kicking their chairs away as they did so like a cartload of chimpanzees.

"See you soon, Harrison." Craig said as he walked out of the pub.

Harrison watched them leave and exhaled, realising he had been holding his breath since Blake had walked in.

Blake gave him a supportive squeeze on the shoulder. "It's alright Harrison. They're not going to touch you."

"I don't encourage trouble like that, officer." Robin said cautiously. He had been wiping the same glass for the past five minutes and it was starting to develop streaks.

"I'm sure you don't. Pint please.

"I'll get that if you want." Harrison offered.

Blake shook his head. "No thanks Harrison. Thank you, but no."

"I only wanted to thank you for getting them off my case."

"And I appreciate that."

"And," Harrison continued imploringly. "You did say that I could get in contact with you."

"Yes, I know I did," Blake said, glancing at Robin. "But I meant when I'm on duty. If you want to talk about anything, then come by the station tomorrow. But I can't talk about anything to do with the case with you other than that."

Harrison nodded sadly and walked out of the pub. He stood in the doorway as he watched Craig and his friends disappear in the opposite direction.

Maybe he would go to the police station tomorrow. He certainly couldn't discuss how he was feeling with his parents and Blake just seemed to understand how people felt in these situations, though he now felt incredibly stupid and embarrassed for offering to buy Blake a drink. He put his hands in his pockets and started the long walk back to Halfmile Farm, hoping that by the time he got back his father would have gone to bed.

Blake sighed as he watched Harrison leave. He knew he was doing the right thing but he wanted nothing more at that moment than to run after Harrison and bring him back. He looked absolutely desperate. Sometimes he wished that there weren't such stringent rules that he *had* to abide by. But sitting down and having a drink with, whether he agreed with it or not, a main suspect in a murder investigation would lead to not only the case being completely and utterly tarnished but him losing his job. Sometimes he had to have almost robotic emotions.

Robin placed the pint in front of him and Blake handed his money over. "You're the new guy that started then?"

Blake raised his eyebrows. Was the area really that quiet that the appointment of a new D.S was common knowledge?

"Yeah, that's right." He said. "Who was that lad exactly?"

Robin looked towards the door. "Who, Craig?"

"Yeah, the one that was giving Harrison trouble."

"Craig Samuels." Robin replied, reaching for another glass to wipe. "He was an old school mate of Daniel Donaldson's."

"Ah." Blake said, sipping his pint.

"They've been knocking about together for as long as I've worked here."

"Are you the landlord?"

"Yep." Robin said proudly, holding the glass up to the light. "Ten years this August."

Blake nodded. "Well, congratulations. They're not the easiest of places to run."

"Oh it's not too bad round here." Robin said. "The most trouble I've had, as it happens, is from Craig and Daniel."

"Oh?"

"Yeah." Robin placed the glass back and leaned against the bar.

"There's been a few times when they'd been in here being, well, you know. Boisterous shall we say? They used to go boxing together and you know what lads like that can be like. Had to ring you lot a couple of times. They got taken in for a night or two for, what you call it, drunk and disorderly."

Blake nodded again as he thoughtfully sipped his pint. He wondered that if Craig and Donaldson were such troublemakers that it meant that Daniel had managed to accumulate a few enemies up to his death.

"You must get to see quite a lot of the village's laundry being the local landlord?" Blake asked, pulling his ecig out of his pocket. "Do you allow this in here?"

"Yeah, as we're quiet." Robin said, waving a hand. "You could say that, yes. I mean, the Donaldsons, they've got a fair few stories to tell as a family."

"Go on?" Blake offered, sucking the ecig, being careful not to blow the vapour in Robin's direction.

"Well, they weren't too bad before Brian, that's the dad, was killed in that car crash."

"Daniel's dad?"

"Yeah. Oh that was just tragic." Robin sighed. "I remember the night it happened, he'd been in here. He was in a proper state. He said he'd been arguing with his missus, Helen, that's Daniel's mum. I mean she's always had problems with drink and, well. Other stuff, you know."

"Drugs?"

"Well, I don't know for sure." Robin said, holding his hands up. "But that's what everyone thinks. Anyway, that night Brian was in here and was really knocking them back. In the end, I had to tell him he'd had enough. Course, I didn't know that he then got into his car. Took a bend too fast and that was that."

Blake shook his head. He had very little sympathy for anybody who got behind the wheel of a car in that state.

"Turned out he'd been on his way to see this other woman. I don't know who she was. But, safe to say she was a bit on the side. Anyway, the family just sort of broke down after that. Helen got worse, the daughter, oh what's her name, Vicky. She got arrested and locked up for breaking into Jai Sinnah's corner shop and beating him up. And now with this horrible business with Daniel, well. I dread to think what this will do to them. It's just been disaster after disaster for them."

According to Patil, when Blake had briefly spoken to her on their way back from Halfmile Farm, Helen Donaldson had been just as unresponsive as Gardiner had said she would be. She had apparently been lying face down on the sofa when Patil had arrived, an empty bottle of vodka lying on the floor next to her.

Patil had spent most of her time there trying to stop her from choking on her own vomit.

Blake shuddered. He had seen plenty of families disintegrate like that over the years and it unnerved him as to how easy it was for it to happen.

Blake spent another hour or so in the pub before deciding to call it a night. He had managed another two pints before leaving and as the crisp night air hit him as he zipped up his coat outside, he realised he was actually feeling quite drunk. It was hardly surprising as he had not eaten since Jacqueline's breakfast that morning and had had a couple of broken hours sleep the night before at the most.

As he wandered home, he saw a young man and woman kissing in the threshold of one of the houses. She giggled coquettishly into his ear and as Blake approached, she opened the door and they both disappeared into the house, the door slamming shut behind them. Blake rolled his eyes cynically. He remembered a date Nathan and he had been on that had ended in a similar manner, except they literally had fallen into the house and Blake had ended up nearly cracking his head open on a coffee table. It should have been a sign in retrospect but Blake had always worn rose tinted glasses as far as Nathan was concerned.

As he arrived home, his mind returned to the wedding invitation that was currently in pieces on his living room floor somewhere and a huge surge on indignation soared through him. Why would Nathan do that? Was it not bad enough that he had broken his heart? Forced him to move away from everything he knew? No, he felt that he had to rub it in a bit more by asking Blake to watch him get married to somebody else.

Blake slammed the door behind him and flung himself into the chair in the living room, pulling his phone out of his pocket. He wanted to speak to Sally so that she could talk some sense into him, make him laugh or at the very least bring him back from the conclusion that all other men were the scum of the earth.

But as he flicked through his phone book, he came to the 'N's. Nathan's name and number stared at him. Before he could stop himself, his thumb had hit the call button.

CHAPTER
TEN

The next morning, Blake darted into the living room. He was running late for work. He looked around everywhere for his shoes that he had apparently kicked off his feet with drunken wild abandon the night before. His head was throbbing. How had he gotten so drunk on three pints of beer? Could he really not handle his alcohol anymore? He saw one of his shoes poking out from the coffee table and thrust the wrong foot into it. He decided that he blamed the countryside. Even its beer didn't agree with him.

He finally found his other shoe and quickly

finished getting changed, glancing at the clock as he did so. He had ten minutes to get to work and his hangover was feeling worse with every passing second. He felt like he had the morning after consuming all those gins with Sally before he left. He pushed the terrifying thought that he was getting older out of his head and started trying to focus on what he was going to do that day.

The first thing he wanted to do was speak to Craig Samuels. He got the feeling that he could shed more light on what Daniel Donaldson got up to when he wasn't with Harrison better than anybody else. Harrison ticked all the boxes of the victim in the typical domestically violent relationship – did what he was told, took the beatings and asked no questions. It always saddened Blake when it was just as simple as that. The abusers were able to do whatever they liked and come home knowing that they could smack any guilt out of themselves and onto their partner.

Someone had been pushed to their limits though. There was somebody out there who Daniel Donaldson had gone too far with and he was now laying in a mortuary for his troubles. The problem with people like Donaldson wasn't the lack of motive from anybody, it was finding the culprit who felt they had more motive than everybody else and then, in this case, managing to kill him in such an impossible way. The thought of trying to work out exactly how made his head hurt even more.

He patted his pockets looking for his mobile then saw it lying on the floor by his living room chair. Immediately a flashback from the night before hit him. Closing his eyes in dread he picked it up and looked at the screen. A voicemail message was waiting to be heard. He sighed, then played his messages:

'One new message. Received today at 7:33AM.'

The next voice was an angry sounding Irish one he knew all too well.

'I'm guessing your head hurts quite a lot today and you know what? Good. Who the hell do you think you are, calling me up and hurling abuse on my answer phone? You're a mess when you're drunk, do you know that Blake? Yeah, you're hurt, but do you know what? Big deal. Grow up. You can just tear up that wedding invite because –'

He didn't need to hear any more. He deleted the message and groaned loudly. Despite the severity of his hangover, he remembered every word he had ranted into his phone last night and very little of it had been polite, in fact most of it had been borderline abusive. Nathan's accent had always been one of the things

Blake found most attractive about him but it had been the last thing he wanted to hear that morning.

Stuffing his phone into his pocket with a heavy sigh, Blake thrust his foot into his other shoe and went to work.

Blake's mind whirred as he drove towards Craig Samuels's car garage on the outskirts of the village. His hangover was mercifully starting to dissipate but the fogginess in his brain was still there, as was the feeling of what a complete idiot he was for ringing Nathan. It would probably be a good idea to delete his number so he didn't end up giving a repeat performance.

"Sir? I think we just passed it."

"Hm?"

Blake looked in the rear view mirror as the garage rapidly got smaller behind them. "Oh, was that it? Not very big, is it?"

"Nothing is round here Sir." Patil laughed.

When he had finally arrived at work, Mattison and Gardiner had already been sent out to deal with some trespassers further up the hill so Patil was left as his accompanying officer to interview Craig Samuels. After yesterday, Blake had been relieved to work with somebody new. Patil seemed bright and capable and had asked Blake lots of questions about the case before they'd set off so that she was fully up to speed and Blake felt that she had genuinely taken it all in. If

Gardiner was the odd one out in a station full of officers like this, then Blake felt he could probably cope fine in the long run.

"Have you had many run-ins with our young Mr Samuels?" Blake asked Patil as he parked the car near the garage.

"A couple." Patil said. "Mainly just being drunk and disorderly. You'll get to know who to keep an eye on for what around here before too long."

"Was he ever with Daniel Donaldson?" Blake asked her as they got out of the car.

"Only once." Patil replied. "They were giving a couple of guys a bit of trouble outside The Dog's Tail one night. It was Craig mostly though."

The first thing they saw as they walked into the garage was a pair of legs sticking out from underneath a Peugeot 204. Blake cleared his throat. "Craig Samuels?"

The sound of metal tinkering underneath the car stopped. The figure underneath the car pulled himself out and looked up at them

"Yeah?" He snarled.

"Craig, we'd like to ask you a few questions about your friend Daniel Donaldson?"

"Go on then."

"Could you sit down?"

Craig rolled his eyes then threw the spanner he was holding on the floor, got up and went and sat down at the desk leaning back arrogantly in the chair. "Go on then."

"How well did you know Daniel?" Blake asked him.

"I grew up with him pretty much." Craig replied. "Went to the same school."

"You went boxing with him didn't you?" Blake said, leaning back against the car with his arms folded.

"Yeah, for a bit. He was better with his fists than me though."

"Yes." Blake leant back in a similar fashion to how Craig was sitting. "So we've been led to believe."

Craig scowled at him. "What's that supposed to mean?"

"How much do you know about his relationship with Harrison Baxter?"

Craig narrowed his eyes, then shrugged. "I knew they were…you know."

"What?" Blake asked innocently.

Craig glared at him sullenly. "I knew they were together."

"Did Daniel ever talk to you about any aspect of the relationship?"

Craig shrugged again. "Like what?"

"Like any violence in the relationship?" Blake offered.

Craig didn't answer. He just scowled and once again shrugged.

"Craig?"

Craig glared at Blake. "Yeah, I suppose. I didn't know that much though."

"Did you ever see Daniel hit Harrison though?" Patil asked.

Blake could see, despite the bravado, that Craig was feeling distinctly uncomfortable.

"Look," He snapped. "I'm not gonna sit here and slag off one of my best mates, especially as he only died yesterday."

"I'm not asking you to slag him off," Blake replied. "But this is a murder inquiry so I'm afraid we need to know whatever you knew about Daniel so that we can find out who did this to him." Craig sighed huffily. "So." Blake repeated, slowly. "Did you ever see Daniel hit his boyfriend?"

There was a long pause before Craig gave another sulky shrug. "Yeah, I suppose."

"Yeah, you suppose." Blake nodded, standing up from the car and walking across the garage towards him. It wasn't like him to use intimidation tactics when interviewing a potential witness, but he rather got the impression that Craig didn't think that the domestic violence was a major issue because it wasn't between a man and a woman. He leant against the desk Craig was sat at and looked down at him. "How many times did you see Daniel be violent towards Harrison?"

Craig looked up at him, jigging his leg up and down in an agitated fashion. "A couple of times."

"What did you see?"

Craig sighed, apparently deciding to be truthful so as to get this awkward line of questioning out of the way. "First time we were out at the Tail -"

"The Dog's Tail public house?"

"Yeah."

"Go on."

Craig shifted in his seat. "We'd had a bit to drink, me and Dan. Actually, Dan was wasted. Harrison was whining on about needing to get back so that his Dad didn't have a go at him or something and Dan, I dunno, he just lost his temper."

"So what did he do when he lost his temper?"

Craig looked down at the ground, his leg bobbing up and down again. "When we got outside, Dan pushed him against a wall by his head and told him to shut up. Then he shoved him away again."

"Was that all that happened?"

Craig hesitated. "That time, yeah."

"And the second time?" Patil asked him, crossing her arms.

"Look," Craig said standing up. "I don't know anything about how he was killed. If you think that Dan knocking his *boyfriend* about is that important, shouldn't you be bothering him instead? I've got work to do today!"

"Yeah and you can get on with it when we've finished asking our questions." Blake replied. "So, sit down?"

Craig muttered to himself moodily and then sat down again. It was like trying to ask a teenager to do the washing up.

"What happened the second time?"

There was a long pause before Craig finally said "You know those break- ins at the farm?"

Blake frowned. "Yes? What do *you* know?"

"Look, I don't know all that much. But I think Dan might have known the lads doing them."

"And what gives you that idea?"

"I went to meet him one night before boxing. Dan and Harrison were arguing about something as I was walking towards them. Harrison said something like…I dunno…'*do you know who's doing it?*' Or something like that."

"And he was talking about the break-ins?"

"I don't know for sure. But then Dan had his hand round Harrison's neck and was all like '*That's between my mates and your dad,*' or something."

Patil and Blake looked at each other. "Why would it be between Dan's mates and Seth Baxter?" Blake asked, confused.

Craig shrugged. "How should I know? I don't even know if that's what they were talking about."

Blake bit his lip and thought. Was it possible that

Seth had arranged for some of Daniel Donaldson's friends to break into his farm? Why would he do that?

"Look, I've told you all I know." Craig snapped sulkily. "Can I do my job now?"

Blake looked down at him thoughtfully. "For now, yes. We'll be back if we have anything else to ask you though. Don't plan any trips anywhere."

Craig retorted sarcastically but Blake wasn't listening, instead strolling out of the garage and pulling his ecig out of his pocket. Was he on the right train of thought here? He leant against the car and stared in the distance, inhaling on his vape.

"Sir?" Patil said as she approached him. "What do we make of that?"

"Did you get from that that Seth Baxter arranged for his farming equipment to be stolen?"

"Sounded like it." Patil nodded. "If that's what Harrison and Daniel were talking about when Craig overheard them."

"But he built that shed in response to those break-ins." Blake frowned, thinking out loud. "He built the shed that Daniel Donaldson was somehow shot in to keep people from stealing his equipment."

"So if he wanted the thefts to happen, why build the shed?" Patil pondered.

"Well." Blake murmured thoughtfully. "Either I'm being incredibly dim or Seth Baxter has been incredibly clever. Or possibly both."

They climbed inside the car and Blake started the engine. They needed to get back to the station so that he could fully chew this over. Things were starting, very slowly, to add up.

CHAPTER
ELEVEN

Harrison was sat in an interview room at the police station with his head in his hands. No sooner had he woken up that morning, praying that the day ahead would be easier than the one before, Gardiner and Mattison had arrived at the house, asking him to come down to the station to *'assist with their enquires.'* Despite Sandra's protests, Gardiner had led him to the police car and driven him here, without giving him any indication about what they were going to ask him. All Harrison knew was that Gardiner wasn't anywhere close to being as comforting and reassuring as Blake. In fact, he rather felt like he was being treated like a suspect.

His thoughts were broken when the door to the interview room opened and Gardiner and Mattison entered.

Gardiner sat at the table and glanced up at him. "Sorry to keep you waiting." He said, not sounding in the slightest bit apologetic at all.

Harrison didn't reply. Gardiner leant across the desk and pressed a button on a tape recorder that was lying on the far side.

"Interview commencing at 11:34, present in the room are PC Michael Gardiner and PC Billy Mattison. Also present is Harrison Baxter."

Harrison glanced at Mattison who just looked down at the floor.

"Ok, Harrison. We'd like to talk to you about the shooting of your partner, Daniel Donaldson." Gardiner began.

"Well, we weren't together anymore." Harrison murmured.

"When did you break up?" Mattison asked gently.

"Erm," Harrison shifted in his seat. "Well, to be honest I'd just broken up with him when it happened."

"So the same day he was killed?" clarified Mattison.

Harrison nodded.

"For the tape please?" Gardiner said sharply.

"Yes."

"So, why did you break up with him?" Gardiner leaned back in his chair with his arms crossed.

"Well, he'd been hitting me."

"So your relationship was violent?"

"Yeah."

"How long were you together?"

"About four years." Harrison replied.

"And for how long was the relationship violent?" Mattison asked him.

"For about two years."

"And was he violent towards you very often?" Gardiner didn't sound in the slightest bit sympathetic. Harrison wasn't even sure if he believed him. In some ways, Gardiner reminded him of Daniel. He had that same standoffish nature with just a hint of unpredictability.

Harrison nodded timidly. "Quite often yeah."

Gardiner shrugged. "Was there ever any witness to these attacks?"

Harrison thought back. The only person Daniel had ever been violent towards him in front of was Craig Samuels and he doubted that Craig could be relied upon to give him any support in the matter.

"Not really no. It all tended to happen when we were alone."

"So, just your word against his then?" Gardiner

said, a hint of condescension in his voice.

Harrison glared at him. "Oh I've got proof." He stood up and forcefully pulled up his t-shirt to reveal his bruises. "Look at me. This is what he did to me for two years! Whenever he felt angry or sad or even probably happy I got a new bruise to add to the collection!"

Mattison gave Gardiner a reproachful look then said, "For the tape, Harrison is showing us a series of bruises and marks on his lower body. Did Daniel give you all of those bruises?"

Harrison pulled down his t-shirt again and sat, taking a deep breath to calm himself, then nodded.

"For the tape." Snapped Gardiner.

Harrison sighed. "Yes!"

Gardiner appeared to suck on his teeth thoughtfully. "Except, having spoken to your mother, you told her that you received those marks and bruises from an attempted mugging in the village?"

"No," Harrison exclaimed desperately. "I told her that at first because she saw them and I hadn't told anybody about what was happening. She knew though, I told her the next day."

"You told her the truth about Daniel being violent towards you, the next day, just before he was murdered?" Gardiner asked.

"Yeah."

"So why didn't you tell anybody about it sooner?

You say you broke up with him because of how he'd been treating you, so why did it only happen yesterday?"

Harrison tried to think of a response but he genuinely didn't have one. "I don't know."

"You don't know why you didn't tell anyone or you don't know why you only broke up with him yesterday?"

"Either!" Harrison cried desperately. "Both! I don't know!"

Gardiner leant across the table towards him like a viper about to strike its prey. "So you break up with him and then, what, half an hour later, he's found shot in a locked shed. He didn't have the best of days, did he?"

Harrison didn't respond.

"So, let's talk about how he actually died." Gardiner opened the folder he had been carrying and produced a series of forensics' photographs. Harrison looked at them and winced. They were all of Daniel, lying face down on the ground.

"Shot, three times. Bullet wounds in three separate areas of his body." Gardiner said slowly as he laid the photos out deliberately in front of Harrison. "Except that he was found shot in a shed that nobody could possibly have got in or out of. So, how did that happen?"

Harrison stared at him horrified. "I don't know!"

"Except here's where we've got a problem." Gardiner glanced across at Mattison, as if to insinuate that he felt the same. "We have CCTV footage – from cameras that were put up by your father – of Daniel being locked in the shed, again, by your dad. He's alive when he goes in. Only one other person goes anywhere near that shed between him being locked in it and his body being discovered by us."

Harrison nodded. "Yes, I know that."

"You." Gardiner added unnecessarily. "You walk towards the shed and go round the side, out of view of the camera."

"I was just talking to him."

"See," Gardiner leant back triumphantly. "You say you were only talking to him but, from where I'm standing, logically, you're the only person who could have shot him."

"I didn't!"

"So how did you do it?"

"I didn't shoot him!"

Gardiner leant forwards again, looking angrier. "Oh come on Harrison! Nobody else could possibly have done it."

"Look, I know!" Harrison cried desperately. "I know, but I *swear* to you – I don't know how he was killed, I promise!"

Gardiner paused dramatically then stood up and paced around the room. Despite how emotional he was feeling, Harrison couldn't help noticing that Gardiner looked like a complete idiot doing it.

"When we arrived at the farm," Gardiner said finally. "We heard the sound of a gun being fired." He finished his pacing around as he arrived behind Harrison. "Didn't we?"

"Yes."

"Now, we know that one gunshot doesn't produce three bullets don't we?"

"Yes."

"So where did that gunshot come from?"

"I don't know."

"Help me out here Harrison, I don't think you understand how serious this is."

"Of course I do." Harrison was having difficulty keeping his emotions in check. Any minute now he could feel himself starting to cry again and he didn't want to give Gardiner the satisfaction. "But I was standing with you when we heard it so how could it have been me?"

"You tell me." Gardiner replied. "When we've got people getting shot in locked rooms, I'd say anything's just about possible, wouldn't you? And if it wasn't you who could it have been?"

Harrison looked desperately across the table at Mattison but he just stared back at him as if pleading with him to come up with a reasonable alibi. "I don't know." Harrison said softly.

A look of triumph was now on Gardiner's face. "I do." He leant down so that he was standing over Harrison. "And, let's be honest, so do you. Now I'm going to give you one last chance at making this whole sorry mess that little bit easier for yourself. How did you kill Daniel Donaldson?"

Harrison was at a loss for words. Would confessing to something he hadn't done make things easier for him? It was pretty clear that all the evidence the police had pointed to him and he couldn't think of anything else to defend himself. Maybe, if he ended up in court, the judge would be sympathetic because of how the relationship had been?

But before he could say anything, the door to the interview room opened. Gardiner's head snapped up furiously at the new arrival. Mattison looked relieved.

Blake was standing in the doorway, staring levelly at Gardiner. He glanced at Harrison and walked into the room.

"Interview suspended at..." He glanced at his watch. "11:51." He flicked the tape, stopping the recording.

Harrison glanced up at Gardiner who looked absolutely incandescent with rage. "What do you think you're doing?"

"Yes, *really* sorry to interrupt," Blake smiled, cheerfully. "But I just need a quick word. It won't take long, I promise. Can I just borrow you?"

Gardiner stared at Blake with furious disbelief.

"Sorry Harrison, we'll try not to keep you too long." Blake said as he opened the door again. "Alright Matti?"

"Sir." Mattison grinned back.

Gardiner stormed furiously out of the room and Blake closed the door behind them.

CHAPTER
TWELVE

Blake walked a little further down the corridor away from the interview room. He rather suspected he was going to get another reprimanding from Royale for what he had just done so his immediate priority was trying to get Gardiner on side before he could go any further.

"What the hell do you think you're doing?" Gardiner hissed. "I am in the middle of an interview."

"Yes, I know, I was listening." Blake said hastily. "And before I go any further, I want to tell you that I'm very impressed with your interviewing techniques.

Great stuff to show Mattison!"

"If I'm that talented, then why did you stop the interview?"

"Because Patil and I have just got back from talking to Craig Samuels." Blake replied. "Now, he seems to think he overheard Daniel telling Harrison that he had had something to do with the break-ins at Halfmile Farm, courtesy of Seth Baxter."

Gardiner frowned. "And this removes Harrison as a suspect because?"

"Look, the shed that Daniel was found in was built by Seth, yes?"

"Yes."

"So, if Seth was basically arranging for his own farm to be looted, why the hell did he need a shed to keep all his equipment in?"

Gardiner exhaled, apparently calming down slightly. "So, you know this for a fact, do you? I mean, do you have evidence to support this?"

"Not a hundred percent, no." Blake replied. "But I need to ask Harrison what Daniel said to him that Craig overheard."

"Look, I don't -"

"– Michael, I need us to be on the same page with this. Just let me ask Harrison what I need to and if what I'm thinking at the minute doesn't come to anything then -"

"- Then I can continue getting my confession out

of him, uninterrupted by you?" Gardiner clarified waspishly.

Blake resisted the urge to come back with something more acerbic and merely nodded with what he hoped was a genuine smile on his face.

Mattison walked out of the interview room and towards them. "What's going on?"

Blake turned to face him. "Right Matti, I need two things. Number one, get onto forensics and see if they've come back with anything from the CCTV footage of the shed. I know it's a long shot but any cuts in the film that they think have somehow been spliced together or something?"

"OK," Mattison nodded keenly.

"Second, I want you to find out everything you can on Seth Baxter."

"Well, he's ex-army for one thing." Gardiner said with a hint of approval.

"Good! Good." Blake exclaimed, his brain whirring. "Anything you can find out about that then, his rank, what corps he was in, anything. OK?"

"Yes, Sir."

"Ask Patil to help you if needs be!" Blake called after him as Mattison disappeared down the corridor.

"Will do!" Mattison called back, briefly turning round to show a big grin on his face.

Blake smiled to himself and then turned back to Gardiner. "Right, I think we've let Harrison stew quite enough now, don't you?"

Gardiner just shrugged begrudgingly.

"Right then Harrison." Blake said as he walked back into the interview room. "Really sorry to keep you waiting. I've just got a few questions I need to ask you."

Harrison sighed, looking slightly desperate, though he looked a lot calmer than he had when Blake had interrupted the interview. "I've told you everything I know."

"Yes, I'm sure you have." Blake smiled. "It's not just Daniel I want to talk to you about though."

Harrison frowned in confusion as Blake leant across the desk and pressed the recorder on. "Interview recommenced at 12:05pm. Present in the room is myself, Detective Sergeant Blake Hart, Detective Constable Michael Gardiner and Harrison Baxter."

He leant across the table with his hands clasped together. "Harrison, I want to ask you about your Dad."

Harrison looked surprised. "My Dad?"

"Yeah. Tell me about him."

Harrison shrugged. "There's not much to tell. He used to be in the army for years. Dad's always said he came to the countryside for a quieter life after all the craziness of the gunfire and destruction and everything. I don't know how he did it. It sounds like my worst nightmare."

"Yeah, mine too." Blake said gravely. "Do you get on? You know, as father and son?"

Harrison thought for a moment. "Me and Dad are different I guess you could say. He's big and butch and swears a lot and watches football and stuff like that. The whole thing about me being…"

Harrison glanced at Gardiner nervously.

"Gay?" Blake offered.

Harrison looked down at the table. "I don't think it was very easy for him to deal with. Mum was alright with it – she said she'd always known."

"Mums do." Blake grinned.

"But Dad, it was like he switched off for a few weeks. He didn't really talk to me for ages. Don't get me wrong, he didn't get angry at me or anything but I don't think he was happy, put it like that."

"So when you introduced him to Daniel for the first time, what happened?"

"Not a lot to be quite honest. Mum obviously knew about it before Dad did. For the first couple of months, Daniel was just a mate as far as Dad was concerned. I guess it helped that Dan didn't exactly come across as, well, what Dad thought a gay guy would be like, anyway."

Blake nodded.

"Then one night, I got the courage to tell him. Daniel had been pushing for it for ages. I think he was getting a bit sick of having to be secret all the time. I remember Dad was doing some metal work in one of the old barns and I just walked in and told him."

"And what did he say?"

Harrison gave a humourless laugh. "Not a great deal. He just said something about it being my choice and then carried on hammering this bit of steel."

"So, you'd come out to both your parents and then, what? You're in this happy relationship?"

Harrison nodded and looked down at the table again. "Then, when Dan's dad died, he just changed. From that day onwards it was like he was a completely different person. He started hanging out with Craig Samuels more and..." His voice trailed off, a hint of sadness exuding from him.

"And then the violence started?" Clarified Blake.

"Yeah." Harrison said quietly.

There was a brief pause as Blake considered how to phrase his next question. "Harrison, I want to ask you about the break-ins at the farm."

Harrison looked up at him surprised. "Why?"

"Do you have any idea who was behind them?"

Harrison glanced at Gardiner and then back to Blake. "Well, no, not really."

"But you know a little bit?" coaxed Blake. "It's OK." He said when Harrison hesitated. "You're not in trouble for this, but I just need to know."

"Daniel said something once. He'd been acting

really weird whenever I brought it up and then one day I just came straight out with it and asked him if he knew anything." Harrison sighed. "We'd be arguing about something or other and he was a bit drunk and, well, to be honest I thought he was just trying to threaten me or something. But he said *'That's between my mates and your Dad.'* I didn't get to ask him anything else, Craig came to meet him and they went off together."

Blake looked over, a little triumphantly at Gardiner. "So, he said that his friends had something to do with the break-ins?"

"Well, yeah." Harrison murmured. "I don't think he meant it though. I mean, that wouldn't make any sense would it? Why would Dad get his own property stolen?"

Blake gave Harrison a small smile and leant across the desk to the tape. "Interview terminated at 12:20pm."

"What happens now?" Harrison asked, a look of worry in his eyes as if Blake was about to throw him in a cell.

"You go home." Blake replied. "If we need anything else, we'll let you know. Will you be alright getting home?"

Harrison seemed surprised but relieved. "Yeah. Yeah, I'll be fine."

"Good." Blake smiled, shuffling some of the

papers that were on the desk. "Michael, could you show Harrison out?"

Gardiner glared at Blake then stood up and gestured towards the door. Harrison stood up, thanked Blake and then left the room. Gardiner threw one last annoyed look at Blake then followed

Harrison out of the room, slamming the door behind him.

As soon as the door had closed, Blake was able to be alone with his own thoughts at last. He felt that the interview with Harrison had confirmed what he had already suspected. There was absolutely no doubt in his mind that Seth Baxter had arranged the break-ins at the farm and he also suspected he knew why. The break-ins would all be so very inconsequential if it wasn't for the murder and the fact that it was performed in such an impossible way. Blake was sure that the fact that Daniel Donaldson was shot with apparently no way of it being achieved was nothing more than an elaborate alibi. Like all good magic tricks, the solution, he was sure, would be found in what he hadn't seen as opposed to what he had.

The CCTV footage had shown Seth throwing Daniel into the shed and locking the door, making it impossible to get in or out until it was opened again. So what had gone on in the shed once the door had been locked? Blake suspected that the answer to that was actually very little. There was only one person who could possibly have shot Daniel and it certainly wasn't Harrison.

He needed to speak to Sandra Baxter.

CHAPTER
THIRTEEN

Harrison arrived home with the most bizarre juxtaposition of feelings in his head. Whilst on the one hand he still felt numb and shaken by Daniel's death, anxious, on edge, and extremely sad, he also felt a small glowing deep down that he knew was down to Blake Hart.

Every time he had met Blake now, he had made things better. He had been the one to talk to Harrison one on one after Daniel's body was discovered, he had been the one who had stopped Craig and his gang giving him a hard time at The Dog's Tail and it had been Blake who had stepped in when the interview was really starting to get on top of him. If Blake hadn't had walked into the room when he had, Harrison was pretty sure he would have had a full blown panic attack. In that state he would have confessed to anything to make the feeling of terror he had felt end. So, as silly as it sounded, Harrison almost felt grateful for Blake stopping him from being immediately carted off to face a High Court Judge.

However there were other things about Blake. Whilst the death of Daniel really saddened him, Harrison didn't feel like he had lost a boyfriend. More an old friend that he had lost any respect or admiration for. Daniel had stopped being anything close to a boyfriend a long time ago.

But this was still the first time Harrison had allowed himself to even consider the thought of being attracted to anybody else. Previously, he had always been afraid that Daniel would somehow read his mind and be able to tell he had let his eyes wander. And he found Blake so attractive. From his mousey brown hair that was naturally wavy so that it gave him the sort of quiff that some men spent hours in front of the mirror trying to perfect, to his sepia coloured eyes and slender build. Then there was his genuine and natural smile, which perfectly complimented his handsome face.

Harrison walked up the yard towards the house, glancing at the pair of police officers standing on guard near the shed and the entrance to the farm. Of course all these thoughts were pure and simple fantasy. Blake was the head investigating officer in the murder of his ex-boyfriend – a murder he still felt sure that he was a prime suspect for. There was more chance of Blake starting a relationship with Seth Baxter than there was Harrison. But the fact remained that Harrison hadn't felt this comfortable around a man since he had started going out with Daniel.

He opened the kitchen door to find his mother bustling aimlessly around the room, evidently in one of her kitchen reorganising phases to distract her from the chaos going on around her.

"Harrison!" she exclaimed as he walked in. "Are you alright? What did they say?"

"I'm fine Mum…" Harrison said as Sandra fussed around him. "They just wanted to know about mine and Daniel's relationship, that's all."

"Well, didn't they do that yesterday?" Sandra asked him. "You and that policeman were in here for long enough."

Harrison felt a dull skip in his stomach at the thought of Blake, but ignored it. "Yeah, but they need to be sure of everything I suppose."

"But they don't suspect you of anything?" Sandra asked frantically. "They don't think that you…" Her voice trailed off as she looked at the shed and the officers through the kitchen window.

Judging by the state of her there was absolutely no way she would be able to cope with the suspicion Harrison had that he was the only suspect the police had.

"No, I don't think so."

"Well, that's something at least." Sandra replied, more to herself. She tapped her hands together in an agitated manner as she paced around the kitchen looking for something to clean.

At that moment, his father walked in from the yard and slammed the door behind him. "Bloody police. Why can't they leave us alone? Don't they think we've got enough to deal with without them breathing down our necks all day?"

"They're just doing their jobs." Sandra said soothingly, having found a solitary bit of dust to wipe away in the corner of one of the top cupboards.

"Well, they want to do it somewhere else!" Seth snapped. He rubbed his neck and glared out of the kitchen window.

Harrison glanced up at him nervously and cleared his throat. "Dad?"

"Hm?" Seth grunted, without turning round.

"They were asking me about the break-ins."

Seth's head spun round to look at him. "What break -ins? The one's here?"

Harrison nodded.

"Why?"

"I don't know. Blake, the officer in charge, maybe

thought they had something to do with Daniel."

Seth stormed across the kitchen and leant across the table angrily. "How could they have anything to do with what happened? That's ridiculous. Why would he say that?"

Harrison leant back in his chair defensively. "I don't know. That's just what he asked me."

Seth's eyes narrowed suspiciously. "Why? What did you tell him?"

"Seth, calm down." Said Sandra.

"Nothing!" Harrison replied nervously.

"What did you say when he asked you about the break -ins?"

Harrison looked down at the floor. "Nothing."

"Harrison!" shouted Seth. "*What did you tell him?*"

Harrison looked up at Sandra with a hint of desperation, but there was nothing she could do to help him. She was certainly right when she had said he had never been any good at lying. His father knew there was more to what he had said than what we was revealing.

"Craig Daniels said something to the police about hearing Daniel say something to me about it being something to do with you and him."

Seth's eyes somehow managed to open even wider with fury. "What?"

"Seth?" Sandra asked, shocked. "What do you

mean Harrison? What did Daniel say to you?"

Harrison sighed. "Dan told me that the break- ins were something to do with you and him." He repeated. "I don't know why he said it, but he did. Craig overheard him and said something to DS Harte."

Seth stared at Harrison then at Sandra. He put his hands behind his head and paced the kitchen up and down for a moment.

"Seth?" Sandra asked again. "This isn't true is it? Why would you have anything to do with –"

"And what did you say?" Seth roared at Harrison. "When he asked you – *what did you tell him*?"

"Dad, I couldn't lie, you know I can't. I said that Daniel did say that, but he couldn't have meant anything by it."

Seth let out a frustrated roar, then turned sharply to the window to check on the officers outside.

"Dad, is it true?"

Seth didn't answer. He seemed completely speechless. He merely kept a direct stare with the officers outside.

"Seth!" Sandra said sharply.

"Insurance." Seth replied quietly. "The farm's in trouble. Has been for months. For about a year now."

"What?" Sandra gasped. "Why didn't you tell me?"

"Well what could you have done about it you

stupid woman?!" Seth snapped furiously. "Gone out there and started laying eggs yourself? Came up with some sort of miracle growing formula to make the crops grow faster? I was better off dealing with the situation on my own."

"So you got some of Dan's mates to break in and steal some of the farming equipment?" Harrison clarified. He couldn't quite believe what he was hearing. Seth had always been extremely hostile against Daniel, that is, on the rare occasions where he had even said a word to him.

"That's what I just said isn't it?" Seth grunted.

"Well I have to say I think you've been extremely dishonest and immoral Seth." Sandra scolded. "If you'd just told us the truth, then we could have done something, we could have thought of some sort of solution! What sort of example is that to set to Harrison?"

Seth glared furiously at his wife. Without looking away he said in a dangerously low voice, "Harrison, go upstairs. I need to talk to your mother."

"But Dad I-"

"Now!"

Harrison knew better than to argue with his father when he was in this sort of mood. He hastily stood up and walked quickly out of the room, closing the kitchen door behind him.

When he got to the stairs, he slowed down so that

he could hear what was being said.

"Don't you dare talk to me about setting examples." Seth's voice snapped from the kitchen.

Harrison sat down on the stairs with his head in his hands. He had always hated hearing his parents argue, even from a young age. When they fought like this, it always resulted in –

There was the loud sound of a hand being slapped across someone's face and his mother let out a yelp of pain. Harrison sighed. It had been a long time since he had heard that. Though he had never seen his father be violent towards Sandra, he had heard it plenty of times growing up. His father shouting and yelling insults at her, which would then culminate in the sound of her being kicked, slapped or punched. It had never been spoken about between any of them, apart from when Sandra had seemed to vaguely refer to it to Harrison before Daniel had arrived the previous day.

"Seth!" Sandra's voice sounded strained. "Can't you see? How stupid all of this was?"

Another slap and another cry of shocked pain from her.

"Sandra, stop it. I'm warning you, just stop it." Seth growled.

"But you're going to get caught Seth!" Sandra exclaimed, sounding like she was crying now. "What happens to me and Harrison if you get sent to prison?"

Yet another slap, louder this time. Harrison

pictured his father leaning back with all the force he could muster to deliver a devastating blow to his wife. A large clatter and another strangled cry from Sandra. It sounded like she had been pushed into the table.

Harrison stood up and went to walk towards the door, but as his hand reached the handle, he stopped. He couldn't do it. He just wasn't brave enough. There was no way he would be able to physically stop Seth any more than Sandra could. He rested his head against the doorway and sighed, a tear rolling down his cheek, cursing his own stupid cowardice.

He could hear Seth panting from inside the kitchen. "Just *leave me alone!*" He said forcefully. A moment later, Harrison heard the back door leading out to the yard open and then slam shut. After a brief pause, he heard Sandra sigh heavily and then the sound of the chairs scraping across the floor; presumably picking herself up from the floor after being thrown across the room.

Harrison turned and slowly walked back up the stairs. He had often wondered over the time he was with Daniel why he had put up with the physical abuse after hearing the sort of thing he just had over the years. Maybe it was the fact that Sandra was too scared to try and escape that had made him think there was no way out of his own violent relationship.

All of Harrison's life seemed to have been pivoted around violence in some form or other – his parents, his father towards him on occasions, his own relationship with Daniel, and then ultimately Daniel's death.

He entered his bedroom and lay on the bed, his head aching and his chest tight. He remembered this particular feeling of anxiety from when he was younger – it was a type that seemed to be reserved for when his parents were fighting. He closed his eyes and again tears ran down his cheeks. Despite the fact he had, somehow, seemingly escaped the restraints of his relationship, he had never felt so utterly trapped in his entire life.

CHAPTER
FOURTEEN

"**I** mean what are you, fourteen?"

Blake sat on the wall outside the police station, vape in one hand, mobile phone in the other, smiling to himself as Sally-Ann scolded him. She had heard about his drunken phone call to Nathan the night before and had called to give him her rather candid thoughts on the matter.

"I was drunk." He replied simply.

"Well, that's no excuse!" She replied, amusement in her voice.

"I know, I know. But last night, I dunno. I was

just having a bad time with it all. He sent me an invitation to his bloody wedding Sally. How did he expect me to react?"

"I always said he was an arsehole." Sally sniffed.

Blake laughed. The night before he had walked in on Nathan and his wife to be, Sally had been telling him how Blake and Nathan were the best couple breathing and how she saw their relationship as one that people should take an example from.

"How did you find out anyway?" Blake groaned. "Don't tell me everyone already knows about it."

"You're talking about Nathan here, of course everybody knows about it." Sally replied flatly. "He's also put a Facebook status about it, tweeted it and posted an Instagram picture of you and him with loads of red squiggles all over your face."

Blake rolled his eyes. "As always, the modicum of maturity."

Fortunately, Blake didn't use social media all that much, but he had removed Nathan from Facebook once the vomit inducing photos of him and Cassandra had started to appear.

"So, aside from your messy love life, how are things?" Sally said. He heard a singular click and then the sound of a kettle boiling, meaning that she was at home. "How's small town policing going?"

"Well, it's certainly not been quiet." Blake murmured. "I'd only been here five minutes before I was dealing with this really weird murder case. I'll tell you all about it when I've got some more time but it's not like anything I've come across before."

"See?" Sally exclaimed over the sound of cutlery and cups clattering about. Blake could picture her trying to find a clean mug amongst the pile of washing up in her cluttered kitchen. "And you were worried it would all be graffiti and missing church collection money."

"Sir?"

Blake turned round to see Mattison leaning out of the station doorway.

"I think the boss is ready to start."

"OK, I'll be right in."

Mattison nodded and walked back inside.

"Gotta go. I'll try and ring you later." He said, taking one last suck on his ecig. It was running out of liquid and the residue on the bottom of the tank was leaving a harshness at the back of his throat. "Alright. Have a good day and no more drunken phone calls!"

"I promise, Mum. Love you."

He hung up and walked back into the police station. He would have loved some advice on this case from Sally. At the moment, he did feel like he was kicking ideas about on his own, but he hoped that this meeting would produce a few ideas as to just how Daniel had been killed.

Blake walked into the interview room to find the rest of the team sat waiting for him, with varying degrees of patience. Patil and Mattison were sat at their desks, keenly sat with a pen and their note pads. Gardiner was stood near the whiteboard that had been set up with his arms crossed and Royale was stood in the doorway to his office. A few other officers, some of which Blake hadn't even met yet, were scattered around the room chatting idly with one another. Royale looked up as Blake entered.

"Ah, there you are DS Harte. Right, let's get started shall we?"

"Yes, Sir." Blake replied, throwing his jacket onto the nearest chair. He picked up a marker pen from the tray on the bottom of the board and turned to his audience.

"Right, afternoon everybody. I'd like to start by thanking you all for your work on this case so far. I don't think there's anybody here who wouldn't agree that it's been somewhat challenging to say the least."

"Impossible would be more like it." Sighed Mattison.

Blake nodded. "Certainly seems that way, but the simple fact is that this murder happened, so it clearly isn't impossible. Let's go through what we know."

He picked up his file from his desk and pulled out some photographs, sticking one to the whiteboard.

"First of all, let's take a look at our victim - Daniel Donaldson. Twenty-three years of age. His body was discovered in a locked shed at Halfmile Farm, with three bullet wounds. One in his shoulder, one in his neck and the last one in his abdomen." He indicated on the photograph of Donaldson's body where the wounds were located. "The shed in which he was found had no other ways of entry or escape apart from the door which he entered it by."

Blake picked up a remote control from the desk and pointed it at the television that had been placed next to the white board, a still image of the shed waiting to be played on it.

"As we know, the victim was put into the shed by Seth Baxter." He pressed play and the events played out on the screen, Seth pushing Daniel Donaldson into the shed, locking the door and walking away again.

"Now, the only person who goes anywhere near the shed at any point is Harrison Baxter, ex-partner of the victim." Blake continued as Harrison appeared on the screen. He turned to the board and wrote Harrison's name on it in big bold writing. "We'll move onto him in a moment. Now, Seth claims that he then called the police, which would correspond with the call recorded here at 9:47am. Around twenty minutes later, we arrived. Donaldson is locked in the shed for the entire time. After we have arrived at the farm, we hear one gunshot. The shed is opened and we find Donaldson dead. So, the question is how?"

"You said yourself, Harrison was the only one who went anywhere near the shed before it was opened again." Gardiner replied curtly. He was clearly still annoyed at Blake for interrupting his interview.

"Right, so let's go through that." Blake conceded. He rewound the tape to when Harrison appeared on screen.

They all watched as Harrison tentatively walked towards the shed and then round the side, out of sight of the camera. A few moments later, he reappeared and walked back towards the house.

"He's not there for very long." Noted Patil.

"Long enough to shoot Donaldson though." Gardiner insisted.

"How though?" asked Blake.

"You've never thought he did it though, *Sir*." Gardiner replied shortly, the last word appearing to be said with some difficulty.

"No, I haven't," agreed Blake. "But I am, honestly, more than prepared to listen and consider any theories you have on it. He's out of sight for what, five, ten seconds?"

"There's no way that he could get a gun into that shed." Mattison put in. "We were all there – it's...in...penni...inpenni-"He waved his hand around trying to land on the word.

"Impenetrable?" offered Blake, smiling.

"That's the one."

"Exactly." Blake turned back to Gardiner. "We were all there, we *all* checked that shed over. There's no gaps in the woodwork, no holes, no little trap doors, nothing. Daniel Donaldson was, to all intent and purposes, completely untouchable in that shed. Plus, if Harrison shot him, where did he get a gun from? He hasn't got one in his hands when he goes up and he hasn't got anything when he walks away again."

"The abused partner is statistically -" Gardiner began.

"Yeah, I know that." Blake nodded. "Circumstantially, at the very least, it should all fit together. But this isn't a normal murder case. This happened in a locked shed for God's sake. We're not just trying to work out who, but how. And from what we've seen Harrison, surely, couldn't have done it?"

"There doesn't seem," put in Royale from the office door. "Any way in which anyone could possibly have done it."

"Which means," Gardiner said triumphantly, "that it could still have been Harrison."

Blake sighed, then nodded. "Alright. Fine. So let me ask you this – ignoring any potential suspects for the moment. How? How could he have been shot? How did Daniel Donaldson die in that shed?"

There was a pause.

"Did we discuss the possibility of a remote control device?" Patil ventured. "Something that could have been set off after he'd been locked in there?"

"Well," Blake said, leaning against the desk with his arms folded and looking at the board, remembering Jacqueline suggesting exactly the same thing. "Nothing was found in the shed afterwards that would suggest that that was the case. There was nothing in there except farming and gardening equipment."

"Could they have hidden something in one of the tools?" Mattison shrugged. "I dunno, like one of the hoses or something?"

"Well." considered Blake. "It might be worth having another look round it now forensics have finished in there, but, I don't know. It just doesn't seem likely."

There was another pause whilst Blake considered any other solutions to the puzzle, but none came.

"Alright." He said at last. "Let's move on. Now, when we arrived, we heard that one gun shot. Obviously, Donaldson's body had three separate bullet wounds in it. So what do we think that's about?"

"A distraction from what was actually happening?" Patil suggested.

"What would it be distracting us from though?" Asked Mattison. "It was a gunshot, which is what killed Donaldson."

"Yes, but." Blake stood up and stared at the white

board for inspiration. "We know that the gunshot we heard was from Seth Baxter's gun that had previously been kept inside the shed. It had nothing to do with what killed Donaldson."

"So, we haven't even got a murder weapon then?" Asked Royale.

"No, Sir." Replied Blake. "But, I'd be willing to bet that when we find it, we'll be able to work out how Donaldson was killed. Alright," He turned back to the room. "Let's talk about Seth Baxter."

"The man you think did it." Snorted Gardiner.

"I haven't said who I think did or didn't do it," Blake retorted, knowing full well that Gardiner was speaking the truth. "But we've got to go through everyone connected to the case, we will discuss Harrison further, I promise. Ok, Seth Baxter. Harrison's father."

He pulled out his marker pen and scribbled on the board. "Now, he was the one who put Donaldson in the shed in the first place. As we've seen on the CCTV footage, he actually frogmarches him in and locks the door. OK, so first question, for me anyway, is why did he put him in this shed?"

"He walks into his kitchen and finds his son being attacked by Donaldson." Patil read from her notes. "He drags Donaldson outside, locks him in the shed so that he can't go anywhere whilst he phones the police."

"Does that not seem a bit extreme to anyone else?"

Blake offered. "Why not just keep him in the house? Lock the kitchen door or something to stop Donaldson from going anywhere? Why does he go to the trouble to lock him inside a shed? Matti, what did you find out about his army life?"

"Erm, well…" Mattison flicked through his notepad. "I would have told you this sooner, but I've not seen you, Sir. For most of his time there, he was a Sergeant in the Grenadier Guards, he was there for twenty years or so."

"An excellent division." Gardiner said approvingly.

"Thank you, Mainwaring." Replied Blake wryly. "Go on, Matti."

"But, before that," Mattison continued. "He did a two year placement in the Royal Artillery."

Blake raised his eyebrows. "Oh did he now?"

"So he'd know his way around a gun and how to handle one discreetly." Patil added.

"Could Seth have shot him on his way to the shed?" Mattison asked, a moment of inspiration appearing in his eyes. He excitedly stood up and walked across the room to Blake and put his hand on his shoulder. "Do you mind being a shooting victim for a moment, Sir?"

"There's easier ways to get a promotion Matti, but go on." Grinned Blake to a ripple of chuckles around the room.

"So Seth is shoving Donaldson across the yard,"

Mattison began, gently pushing Blake into walking across the office. "He then, secretly, pulls out a gun from his pocket…." He slowly and deliberately put his free hand into his pocket and then out again, his fingers now in the shape of a gun. "…Shoots him, then shoves him inside and locks the door?"

There was a pause. Mattison looked at Blake and then the rest of the room for some sort of clarification that he had solved the mystery.

"Yeah, but he'd got three separate wounds on him." Patil said, standing up and tapping the picture on the whiteboard. She then walked across the room and took Mattison's place, her hand now on Blake's shoulder. "The only way he could manage that -Sorry Sir."

"No, go on Mini." Replied Blake. He was delighted that he'd got them thinking of practical solutions. This was the level of involvement he tried to establish in meetings like this.

"The only way he'd manage all three would be really quick handiwork." She marched Blake across the room in the opposite direction, poked him gently in different places to signify him being shot and then pushed him inside Royale's office.

"Even then," Blake said. "*If,* and I do mean *if,*" He added at Gardiner who gave him a resigned shrug of the shoulders. "If we're saying that Harrison didn't do it, then he would have seen Seth do that."

"Unless," Royale pondered. "They were both in it together. Harrison then keeps quiet on the whole thing and his father does the deed?"

Blake sighed, his head beginning to ache. "So, what? Harrison agrees to wait till his boyfriend starts giving him a beating and then they can go ahead with their plan? It just doesn't fit, does it?" He sucked on his teeth, thinking hard. He then smiled at Mattison. "It was a good thought and right now we need as many of them as we can get. I think you're on the right lines Matti, I really do, but we're missing something." He stared at the white board in silence again for a few moments.

"So, who fired the gun that we heard?" Gardiner asked.

"Now that, Michael," Blake said, clicking his fingers and pointing at Gardiner, "Is an excellent bloody question. Let's recap. We're in the yard of Halfmile Farm, Harrison and Seth are standing in front of us, so it couldn't have been them."

"Sandra Baxter claims she was feeding the animals at the time of death." Patil read from her notes.

"Sandra Baxter." Blake muttered, scribbling her name on the white board. He stared at it for a few moments before being struck by a thought.

"What animals have they even got on that farm?"

Gardiner shrugged. "Few hens, couple of sheep I think. The usual farm stock."

"What did we see when we arrived that morning? Chickens that were just scattered all around the farm, a few geese, likewise, that bloody goat and…" His brain whirred. Something wasn't connecting. "There were a few sheep in the distance, near the other end of the field. Have they got anything else? Cows? Horses? Alpaca?" He added dryly.

There were a few shakings of heads and shrugs around the room. "Not that I know of." Replied Mattison.

"Their farm was hit pretty hard by the various flus and epidemics over the past decade." Royale said thoughtfully. "I remember Seth telling me a few months back. Mad Cow's disease, Bird Flu, Swine Flu; they just had really bad luck with it. Doubt they've been able to afford to buy more. They've had very little to sell."

"So, if all of Halfmile Farm's livestock were either in plain sight of us or dead," Blake asked flatly, "Then what the hell was Sandra Baxter busy feeding?"

There was a long silence. Blake's heart fluttered. Had they finally landed on something solid?

"Excuse me, Sir." Blake turned to see Mandy Darnwood standing in the doorway. "Pathology report has come back on Daniel Donaldson."

"Oh, finally." Blake took the report off her and then keenly opened it, his eyes devouring the details.

The sound of a phone ringing from the front desk

echoed around the corridor. "Oh for God's sake." Sighed Darnwood. "I tell you, I've been nonstop in that office today!" She marched wearily out of the meeting room.

"Yeah, the crosswords are longer at the back of her puzzle books." Gardiner muttered, loud enough for everyone to hear and chuckle.

Blake was hardly listening. His mouth was dry, his heart was thumping. He had to reread the same paragraph three times before he assured himself that he had read it right. Ignoring the idle chatter that was going on around him, Blake rewound the tape and watched Seth throw Donaldson inside the shed again. If what the report was saying was right he had just worked out who had killed Daniel Donaldson and how.

"Guys!" Darnwood poked her head round the door again. "Just had a call from Robin at The Dog's Tail, reporting a disturbance. It's Helen Donaldson."

"Daniel's mum." Patil said. "Do you want me to go? I've been her liaison officer throughout this case."

"Yes, good idea Mini." Royale nodded.

"I'm coming with you." Blake called to her as she started to leave. He slammed the folder shut and passed it to Royale. "Have a good read through that, Sir. Matti, Michael. Give me an hour, then I'm going to be back here and we're going back to Halfmile Farm."

"Give it another going over, Sir?" Mattison sighed.

"Nope. Michael, you're going to get your wish."

"And why's that?" Gardiner asked, his eyes narrowing.

Blake pulled his coat off the chair and flung it over his shoulders. As he strode out of the room, he called over his shoulder, "Because I want you to arrest Harrison Baxter for the murder of Daniel Donaldson."

CHAPTER
FIFTEEN

Blake didn't say much as he travelled with Patil towards The Dog's Tail. His brain was whirring with what he had landed on and he was performing a mental checklist in his head to make sure all the facts tallied with what he had realised was probably the only logical explanation of what had happened. There were only a few things he wasn't sure of but he was hoping to be able to iron those out during interviews.

As Patil pulled up at the end of the road, she exhaled through her nose deeply. "She can be a bit of a handful when she's in this state."

"Oh, she's not a spitter is she?" groaned Blake.

Patil merely grimaced and got out of the car. Blake tutted and shook his head as he followed her. It was the only thing that pushed him immediately to the limit and at risk of losing any sense of professionalism. Spitting at someone was just the lowest way to behave as far as he was concerned.

They could hear raised voices as they approached the entrance to the pub, one particularly shrill and abusive female voice by far outperforming the rest. Patil had just put her hand on the door handle when there was a sudden smashing of glass and a bar stool suddenly crashed through the window near where Blake was standing. It landed on the floor with a clatter on the pavement.

"*Right Helen, that's it!*" Roared Robin from inside the pub. "Sod the police, I'll deal with you myself!"

Patil glanced back at Blake who nodded back to let her know he was ready. She then pushed the door open and they found Robin the barman struggling to hold a small, gaunt faced woman in an arm lock. She had streaks of blonde in her extremely messy hair with large areas of black roots showing from beneath and a lit cigarette in her hand.

The pub was a mess. There was broken glass all over the carpet, presumably from glasses that she had thrown across the bar. There was a mirror behind the bar now sporting a large smashed centre and barstools were overturned.

"You seeing this?" Helen shouted at Patil. "You gonna let him do this to me?"

"Robin, let go." Blake said calmly.

"Are you joking?" Snapped Robin, struggling against the force of Helen attempting to get free from his grip. "Have you seen what she's done to this place?!"

"Yes, well we're here now." Blake replied.

Helen kicked her foot back with a huge amount of force against Robin's leg. He howled in pain and let go of her. She immediately made a break for freedom towards the door, but Blake grabbed her as she pushed past Patil.

"That's enough, come on."

She turned round to him and circled her mouth, preparing to spit. In a flash, he put his hand over her mouth. "I promise you that if one single drop of anything leaves your mouth and lands on me then I will personally make sure that you are locked away for any charge I can get you on, and if there aren't any then I will make some up, are we clear?"

She glared resiliently back at him for a few moments and then nodded.

"I mean it." He said slowly and firmly.

His tone seemed to resonate with her and she opened her eyes wider and nodded furiously.

He removed his hand and turned her round to

handcuff her.

"What about all this damage?" Robin said sharply. "I hope you don't think I'm paying for all this!"

"We'll sort it out Robin, don't fret." Patil replied.

"Do you want to get statements from in here whilst I put her in the car?" Blake asked her, turning Helen towards the door. She slumped slightly and he pulled her up straight again.

Patil nodded and Blake frogmarched Helen out of the pub.

She glanced at the barstool on the ground and burst out laughing. "I didn't even mean to do that!" She cackled drunkenly. "I meant it to land against the table but it went flying through the window."

"Yeah and nearly took our heads off at the same time." Blake replied, unlocking the car. "Mind your head." He manoeuvred her into the back of the car and closed the door behind her, before walking round and sitting back in the passenger seat.

"Right then Helen." He began as he slammed the car door. "As you've probably gathered, we're here because you've been reported as being drunk and disorderly, as well as abusive and for damaging public property and general vandalism."

"Like I care." Helen slurred.

Blake nodded. He did feel a twinge of sympathy for the woman behind the grill. She had lost both her children, one murdered and the other behind bars.

Getting drunk was a pretty easy solution to try and numb the pain. "Do you want to tell me how it all kicked off in there?"

"He wouldn't serve me." Shrugged Helen. "I wanted a drink and he wouldn't serve me."

"So you lost your temper?"

"They were all judging me in there." She snapped. "All of them with their beady eyes watching me, the failed mother. Well they don't know *anything* about my life or my kids. All I wanted was a vodka and he starts going "'*Think about what Daniel would have wanted, would he want to see his mum in this state?*' Piss off!"

She kicked the seat in front of her in anger.

"Oi." Blake interjected. "Less of that."

She glared at him, then slumped into the back of the car again.

"This is all that bitch's fault." She growled.

"Which bitch?"

"The bitch," Helen replied slowly. "That took my Brian away from me. Daniel would still be here if it weren't for her."

Blake frowned. "Brian? You mean your husband? Daniel's dad? Why?"

Helen shook her head. "I dunno why you're wasting your time with me, trying to sort me out. There's nothing you can do for me, alright? I'm finished mate. I'm a mess. You should be *out there,* arresting *her*, asking *her* questions about my son's death!"

"Why would whoever your husband was having an affair with know anything about Daniel's death?"

Helen looked up at him disdainfully, an expression on her face that suggested she thought he was being incredibly stupid. "Well, it happened at her farm, didn't it?"

Blake stared at her, his mouth falling open. "Sandra Baxter?"

Helen seemed to physically recoil at the name. "Yeah. *Her*. He was on his way to meet her at some hotel or summit. Then he crashed his car." Furious tears began to appear in her eyes through the smeared mascara. "I didn't even get a chance to tell the bastard how much I loved him."

Blake's brain whirred furiously. "So, just so we're clear. Brian was seeing Sandra Baxter, how long for?"

Helen shrugged, her head leaning drunkenly to one side. "About a year or so I think. Brian told me the night he died. Said I wasn't to start anything. That he was going to end it." She scoffed bitterly. "Like he was going to end it with her. She's a devious cow. She'd have worked on him somehow, got him to keep coming to see her. God, let me tell you. When I smacked her in the face the other day, it felt good. I'd have done it again and again and again, but I only got one in before Daniel pulled me off her."

Blake's mouth went dry. "Daniel knew? About the affair?"

Helen nodded. "Yeah. He knew. Not for very long though. I would have told him after his Dad died but me and him, we argued. Shouted, screaming. I was drinking and..." She shrugged, looking slightly like a child who was being scolded for something. "He didn't want to be around me. Can't blame him I s'pose. He wanted to spend more time with that lad, Harrison. I could hardly take that away from him. Telling him that his boyfriend's mum was the reason things were so bad at home."

Something suddenly clicked in Blake's head. All the questions he had remaining were suddenly getting answered. "So you're the reason Sandra has a black eye?"

Helen threw her head back and let out a cold cackle of laughter. "Yeah. Smacked the bitch right in the face." She demonstrated by whacking the grill between them.

"Did Seth ever find out about the affair?"

"I dunno. Probably not."

"Why did you never tell him?"

"Like I said. I wanted Daniel to be happy. If all of that came out and Daniel lost Harrison, how would that have been fair? I mean, Brian was always really supportive of Daniel being gay, probably dealt with it better than I did. I couldn't take that away from him.

If it had all come out, then I doubt Seth would want him anywhere near his son as a constant reminder of what his wife had been up to."

"Oh, Helen." Blake let his head rest against the window as he took in what he had just be told. "Daniel and Harrison being apart was probably the best thing that could have happened. You do know Daniel had been beating Harrison up ever since Brian's death?"

Helen looked up at him, shocked sadness in her eyes. "No. I never brought him up to be like that!"

"You were protecting him. Or thought you were. You did nothing wrong Helen. In fact you're probably the best mother I've seen in this entire case."

Helen started to cry, sinking down into the seat. As her sobs echoed round the car, Blake's brain started to put the sad truth together. All the lies that Harrison had been led to believe, not only about his own relationship, but that of his parents and all the secrets that had been kept from him. He was positive now who had killed Daniel and who was responsible. And they weren't in any way the same thing. The only way he was going to get a confession however was via a little coaxing.

His thoughts were broken by Patil opening the driver's seat. She glanced across at Helen wailing in the back seat. "I've got the statements, Sir."

"Thanks Mini." He pulled his phone out of his pocket and dialled the station. "Hi Mandy, it's DS

Blake Harte. Can you tell Gardiner and Mattison to bring a car and meet me at The Dog's Tail right away? Cheers." He hung up and sighed, then turned to Patil. "Take her back to the station and put her in a cell for the night." He got out the car, then turned back before he closed the door. "And Mini? Go gentle with her."

Patil frowned, but nodded. Blake watched her drive away, then leant against the wall, his head hurting with the new information. He glanced down and saw a cigarette packet lying on the ground that had presumably fallen out of Helen's pocket on the way to the car. He bent down and picked it up, opening it to find one cigarette and a lighter nestled inside the packet. He glanced around to make sure that nobody was watching, then lit the cigarette and inhaled deeply. His next stop was Halfmile Farm and it was not going to be an easy visit.

CHAPTER
SIXTEEN

Harrison leant against his bedroom window watching the clouds. They had been growing increasingly black as the evening had drawn in and on the horizon they looked almost foreboding. He would have to round all the chickens up if the weather was taking a turn for the worse.

He rubbed his eyes as he shifted to a more comfortable position. He felt exhausted, mentally and physically. His jaw muscles ached fiercely from the anxiety the past few days had brought and his chest kept fluctuating in tightness.

He glanced down at the shed, where this nightmare had all begun. He had tried not to overthink anything about it, but at this moment all he could wonder was what secrets the small building held. Deep down he knew there was only one person who could possibly have killed Daniel and he felt sick at the thought.

As the thought arrived in his head, his eyes darted to the road as flashing blue lights attracted his attention. Two police cars were making their way up the hill towards the farm. He let out a moan of despair. He wasn't sure he could cope with any more questioning.

Before too long, the two police cars were pulling into the yard.

He cautiously watched from his window as Betty ran across to greet the new arrivals. His stomach flipped slightly as Blake climbed out of the car and was gently butted by Betty.

"Why does this goat hate me?" Blake snapped at Mattison.

Gardiner climbed out of the back of the car and immediately glanced up at Harrison. He murmured something to Blake, who looked up at Harrison and grimaced.

Harrison ducked out of view and tried to control his breathing as panic filled up in him. A moment later there was a sharp knock on the door. He heard his father grumbling from the kitchen, then more voices filled the house.

"*Harrison!*" Shouted Seth.

Harrison stood up and took another deep breath. He then opened his bedroom door and hurried downstairs to the kitchen. As he entered, he saw Blake give him a look of what looked like sympathy.

"Harrison." He began. "We need you to come back to the station with us. We've uncovered some new evidence that places you directly in the frame for Daniel's murder."

Sandra and Seth looked at each other in horror.

"What? What evidence?" cried Sandra.

"Evidence that we're very confident will lead to a conviction." Blake replied matter-of-factly. "I take it you're able to get him legal representation? Michael, go ahead."

"Wait," Harrison said weakly. "It wasn't me, I didn't -"

Gardiner smugly stepped forwards. "Harrison Baxter, I'm arresting you for the murder of Daniel Donaldson. You do not have to say anything, though it may harm your defence, when questioned, something you may rely on in court. Anything you do say may be given in evidence." He triumphantly slapped his handcuffs round Harrison's wrists.

"Right, let's go." Blake said, opening the kitchen door. He put his hand on Harrison's shoulder.

"*Dad!* Dad, I swear I didn't do it!" Harrison cried as Gardiner marched him towards the door. But he then felt Blake squeeze his shoulder like he had before, when he had interviewed him in this kitchen. He looked up at him and Blake gave him a brief smile which quickly disappeared.

"You can't do this!" Sandra shouted. "What proof do you have?! Seth, do something!"

Harrison looked desperately across at Seth who seemed rooted to the spot, his brain whirring furiously.

"Seth!" Sandra cried, angrily. "I said *do something!*" She whacked him furiously on the arm.

Seth closed his eyes. "Stop! Please."

Blake blocked Harrison from leaving the kitchen.

"What?" Gardiner snapped. "What's wrong now?"

"You got something to say, Seth?" Blake asked.

Seth looked up at Blake, all fight apparently leaving him. "It wasn't Harrison."

"And how do you know that?"

There was a pause. Harrison turned to look at his father. He looked a former shell of himself. "Because it was me." He murmured quietly. "I killed Daniel."

Blake's expression was unfathomable. "Take the cuffs off him." He said to Gardiner.

Gardiner bristled in fury. "You've got to be joking! Isn't it obvious, he's protecting his son!"

"*Just* undo the cuffs please." Blake said sharply.

Gardiner shook his head in livid disbelief then

166

forcefully removed the handcuffs from Harrison's wrists.

"Dad?" Harrison ventured, barely registering the tightness of the cuffs leaving him. "What are you saying?"

"Exactly what it sounds like." Seth replied. There seemed to be a very small part of him that was relieved. "I'm sorry Harrison. I really am."

Harrison didn't know what he felt more shocked by; the confession or the fact that his father had just apologised to him for the first time in his entire life.

Seth sat down heavily at the kitchen table, staring at the floor.

"That's not a bad idea actually, Seth." Blake said calmly. He indicated to Harrison and Sandra. "Maybe you'd both like to sit down."

Harrison glanced briefly at Gardiner, who looked absolutely furious, then timidly sat down at the far end of the table, Sandra sat opposite Seth and looked up at Blake expectantly.

Blake slowly and deliberately positioned himself against the sink so that he was standing directly in front of all three of them, and took a deep breath, apparently deciding how to phrase what he was going to say.

"There's a lot of sad things I come across in this job." He began. "Things that sometimes don't make the pay packet worth it. Death, destruction, families torn apart either by awful circumstances or by their own design. And this case has brought all of that to the table and then some."

He glanced around at them individually before continuing. "Domestic violence is something that we come across an awful lot. And it never gets any easier to witness and, in a lot of ways, never makes any more sense than the last time you saw it. I mean, who could put their partner through all that? The fear, the pain, the humiliation? And poor Harrison here seems to have been surrounded by it for more years than he cares to remember. Not only in his own relationship, but at home too."

Harrison shuffled uncomfortably in his seat. Seth looked up at Blake but didn't say a word.

"What goes through your mind, Seth? When it's happening?"

Again, Seth remained silent.

There was a pause. Blake crossed his arms, a deep look of concern on his face. "And what goes through *your* mind Sandra, when you're doing it?"

Harrison's eyes widened. He looked across at Sandra who looked horrified.

"I beg your pardon?" She exclaimed, outraged.

"Harrison's told me all about the things he's heard over the years. Heard but never seen. All the fights, all the violence. I'm guessing, after so long, it gets easier? Hitting someone then crying out in pain yourself?

Actually, I'd imagine, in a lot of ways, it's almost therapeutic?"

Harrison's heart seemed to drop out his chest. Blake was right. He had never ever seen his father lay a single finger on his mother. But then, now and again, Sandra had lashed out. Nothing frenzied, not when Harrison was present. But just those occasional moments of anger that he had never picked up on. His mind flew back to earlier in the day when he had heard the argument between his parents and how he had felt so cowardly for not trying to do anything to protect his mother. Exactly what would he have seen if he *had* gone in?

Sandra looked angrier than Harrison had ever seen her. "I don't know who the *hell* you think you are, coming in here throwing awful accusations around like this -"

"Because," Blake continued, ignoring her shouts of protest. "It all actually worked out for you. As an abusive partner I mean. You've got Seth. Ex-army, set in his ways, a real man's man. Even Gardiner here saw you as someone to look up to Seth. And it's not easy to get a compliment out of this one, believe you me." Gardiner rolled his eyes, but said nothing.

"There was no chance on this earth that he was ever going to let it be known by anyone that a woman was beating him up. And there was only one person who he needed to ascertain a sense of authority over.

In his mind, the one person who he needed, to give himself any sense of self-worth, to appear untouchable to. And that was your son. The last thing he wanted was for Harrison to look at him as someone who'd get, quite literally, pushed around by his wife."

Harrison looked across, bewildered at Seth, who hadn't made a sound for the past couple of minutes. "Dad? Tell me this isn't true?"

"Of course it isn't." Snapped Sandra, standing up and pointing angrily at Blake. "I'll be taking you through every court in the land, D.S Harte – you see that I don't."

"Oh, sit down Sandra." Seth murmured.

Sandra stared at him in fury. "Don't you tell me-"

"Or what?" Seth snarled, furiously glaring at his wife. Harrison was stunned to see tears in his eyes. "You'll give me a beating here and now? In front of them? Go on. Show our son what really goes on when the kitchen door is closed. In fact, let's show him how similar me and him really are." He stood up and lifted up his jumper, revealing an almost eerily similar set of bruises on his body to the ones Harrison had tried so hard to keep from his parents. Seth sat down again and glared resolutely at his wife who was temporarily silenced. Seth took a shuddering deep breath.

"I was a fool. An absolute pig headed fool. And a coward. All I learnt when I was in the army was how to defend myself against the enemy. And for what? So that I could make my own son scared of me?" He tried to look at Harrison, but at the last moment couldn't. He simply looked down at the floor. "Son, I'm not proud of anything I've done. Least of all made you live like this all these years. All I wanted was for you to have the life I lost. To be able to stand on your own two feet and to be able to respect people. Turns out I even failed at that."

"Well." Blake said gently. "For whatever reasons you did it Seth, it still wasn't enough for you was it Sandra? Having complete control? So you went looking elsewhere."

Harrison stared at his mother. "Looking elsewhere for what?"

"And that's when Brian Donaldson came on the scene isn't it? From what I've heard, a tall, handsome, younger man who was so different to Seth in so many ways." Blake said, looking at Sandra with a touch of antipathy. "How did you meet? Was it before Harrison started his relationship with Daniel or afterwards?"

Seth let out a humourless chuckle. "You and Donaldson. I *knew* it."

Sandra glared at Seth. Harrison had never seen her look so venomous. "Oh you knew nothing, you stupid man. Brian was the kind of person I should have been with. Sure of himself, with a direction in life. Not just living his last days out on some silly little clapped out farm, hoping that things would improve. Brian was a go-getter."

"You and Dan's dad?" Harrison asked quietly, stunned.

"From what I've managed to ascertain from Helen Donaldson, the affair went on for about a year. Does that sound about right?" Blake asked.

"Oh, she wouldn't know the first thing about what her husband was up to." Laughed Sandra bitterly. "Life was far more interesting at the bottom of a vodka bottle, or whatever other poison she could find to put into her body. Their marriage was over long before I came along."

"And then one night, you were supposed to meet at a hotel?" Blake continued. "And on the way there, Brian crashed his car. The Donaldson's are completely ripped apart. The only stable aspect of their entire family has gone."

Sandra nodded, apparently unaware of anybody else in the room. "Brian had told Helen that night about us. They had a blazing row and he went and got drunk, the stupid idiot. Got in his car and..." Her voice trailed off.

"But," Blake continued. "Helen decided to keep quiet about the affair. The fact was that she knew how little use she was to Daniel. How was she supposed to try and support an angry grieving son when she could barely look after herself? As she saw it, the one positive thing in his life was Harrison. If either he or Seth found out about the affair, that would all be over. So she kept quiet. Until a few months ago."

"Daniel knew?" Harrison asked, completely bewildered.

"Helen had, as usual, had one too many." Sandra sighed, rolling her eyes. "She blurted the whole thing out to him. Daniel came round here in a terrible rage."

"When?" Seth asked, frowning slightly.

"Neither of you two were here thank God." Sandra replied, carelessly. "But the pair of them turned up on my doorstep, hurling all sorts of abuse. I managed to get rid of them, but the damage was done. Unstable woman. She flew for me earlier this week. Whacked me right in the face."

"Resulting in the only black eye your son has ever actually seen you with. Still, your abusive husband could easily be held accountable to that, couldn't he?" Blake said sardonically.

"She told me she'd walked into a door." Seth murmured.

"Well, there's an irony." Blake said grimly. "But now, you're left with a problem. Daniel could, at any given moment, reveal everything to these two. Put simply, you had to get rid of him. So you came up with a plan."

Seth stared at his wife in total disgust. "So that's what all this was about? Keeping your grubby little secret from me?"

Sandra sneered at him. "It was about protecting our son. Brian was the closest thing to a decent human being that family had – what, you think I wanted Harrison to be a part of it?"

"So how did you come to be part of this, Seth?"

Seth looked sadly across at Harrison. "I saw him hit you. He had you pinned up against one of the walls outside and was shouting something at you about being useless and stupid and calling you all sorts."

Harrison remembered it well. That one had hurt. Daniel had ended up throwing him into the dustbins and kicking him in the stomach. And all because Harrison hadn't given him a straight enough answer about what he had been doing that day.

"So, I told Sandra what I'd seen." Continued Seth. "I thought we could do something about it, rather than let Harrison think he couldn't handle it himself."

"Which was the perfect opportunity for you, wasn't it Sandra?" Blake walked across and leant against the table, looking down at her. "And you thought of a way to get rid of him without implicating yourself. The perfect murder. One that couldn't possibly have been committed by anybody that was seen on that CCTV tape, because he'd been locked inside a shed, alone with no way of anyone here being able to get to him."

Blake stood up and looked at the shed through the kitchen window. "Because, that shed was the whole key to this. It was built for this exact purpose. Daniel had started drinking himself by that point and who was to say when he'd become as loose lipped as his mother when he'd had a few? So, between you, but for entirely different reasons, you formulated an airtight plan. But you needed a reason to build that shed and put up all these cameras everywhere that could conveniently act as an alibi for everyone here when the moment came. So, what did you do Seth?"

Seth glanced across at Harrison again, ashamed. "I told Daniel that I wanted him to sort out some break-ins. I knew the sort of lowlife that he hung around with when he wasn't here. I said, money on the farm wasn't coming in and I needed to make cash fast. So, I told him, he'd be able to make a few quid if he could get some of his mates to come in, rough the farm up a bit and steal some of the equipment so that I could call it in on the insurance."

"So," Blake replied. "Once the word has got round, the shed is built, the cameras are up, it's finally time to put this plan into its final stages. So, the big question remains, how did you kill Daniel in a locked shed? Sorry you two, but the mystery sort of collapsed once I'd got the report from the pathologist on Daniel's body. Because in that report, it talked about the bullets used to kill him and the fact that they were incredibly small. Which means, they had to come out of an incredibly small gun. So, once I'd worked that out, I realised there was only one way Daniel Donaldson could possibly have been killed. Is it still in the same place Seth?"

Seth sighed and nodded. Blake's lips thinned and he walked into the living room. Harrison was too shell shocked to say anything.

"This is all your fault Seth." Sandra snarled. "You couldn't even do this right."

"That's enough out of you." Mattison said from the doorway.

Blake returned from the living room clutching something in his hand.

"Essentially," He said. "We have here, what is known in fiction as a classic locked room mystery. But, to be a locked room mystery, the main thing you need is a locked room." With that, he threw what was in his hand onto the table. It landed in front of Harrison with a metal clatter. Harrison stared at the item in front of him. It was the key that normally hung on the hook in the living room.

"We looked into your army background in a bit more detail Seth. Safe to say you spent long enough in artillery to know how to conceal a gun in just about anything. And Harrison happened to mention you were a dab hand at metal work, so creating a key to secure a shed that you've built wouldn't be too much of a trial - and neither would putting a gun in that key that would set itself off when you locked the door."

Blake held up the key so that they could all see it and traced his finger along the rungs at the base of it. "It's designed in such a way that putting this into the keyhole will set it off. Once Daniel was inside, you slammed the door shut. He can't get out and because of the width of that shed, there's absolutely no way he could avoid what was about to happen to him. You fire three times with it, blindly of course, which is why the bullet wounds were in completely separate areas of the body. What Harrison thought was the sound of Daniel trying to kick the door down was in fact the sound of your little gun firing."

There was a long silence in the room. Harrison stared at the key in disbelief. All this time it had been hanging in the living room – exactly how long had it been a gun?

"So, was it planned to be that day? When it happened?" Blake asked.

"No." Replied Sandra. "We were going to invite him round when Harrison wasn't here. I don't think we had a solid plan as such, just that we knew how it was going to be done. But then Harrison said that he was going to break up with Daniel and I -"

"-You realised that if that happened, then Daniel had no reason to keep quiet about what had been going on between you and his father." Blake nodded. "I see. So, you went to find Seth, and told him that it had to happen today."

"She told me Harrison was in danger." Snorted Seth. "That Daniel was most likely going to go mad when Harrison told him that he didn't want to go out with him anymore."

Harrison finally found his voice. "So when you walked in and saw him hitting me, you didn't want to lock him in there to stop him getting away till the police got here, you just wanted to kill him?"

Sandra leant across and tried to take a hold of Harrison's hand. "We did it for you, sweetheart."

"No you didn't." Harrison snapped, pulling his hand away from her. "You just didn't want us to find out about you seeing someone else behind Dad's back!"

"Excuse me," Gardiner said. He had been stood in the far corner of the room whilst all this had been going on, looking graver by every passing minute. "So, what was that gunshot we heard when we arrived all about?"

"I'm sure you could tell us about that Sandra?" Blake asked, raising his eyebrows at her.

Sandra's eyes narrowed and she looked at the floor. "Yes, I used the gun that Seth normally kept in the shed. He got it out of there earlier in the day. Of course the idiot messed that up when he put three bullets into him instead of one."

"Well, it's easily done when you're firing blind. And you're part of it was presumably done to make us believe that we were hearing someone being shot, when in fact it had obviously happened about twenty minutes prior to us arriving."

The silence was confirmation enough. Harrison couldn't hear any more anyway. He stood up and walked out the open front door.

"Harrison, wait!" Sandra cried. But he ignored her. He had no interest in hearing another word from either of them.

He ran outside, but only managed a few yards before he stopped and landed on his knees, dry sobs emanating from his chest. How could this be true? His parents were both responsible for the death of his ex-boyfriend – both of them had lied to him, manipulated him, comforted him in some way since everything had happened and all the time they knew. They knew how he had died and they'd done it for their own reasons. Deep down he had suspected Seth had to have had some involvement somehow. Nothing else had made sense. But his mother, the woman who had been a pillar of support throughout it all had been revealed to be a vindictive, violent and deceitful woman who was only interested in protecting herself, even down to not having the gumption to kill Daniel herself. His father, whilst being a cold blooded murderer had, at least to some degree, been acting on a paternal instinct to protect his son.

Harrison felt a hairy face gently butting the side of

his face. Betty had trotted over and was now nuzzling his ear with either a desire to comfort or eat. Whichever it was, Harrison realised as he tearfully stroked her chin, it was just the two of them now.

CHAPTER
SEVENTEEN

Blake stood in the kitchen doorway, watching Sandra and Seth being led to the waiting police cars. Glancing across the yard, he saw Harrison sat against the wall staring out across the field, Betty grazing the ground next to him. Blake sighed and shook his head. This was one of the worst aspects of the job, seeing people and families trying to pick up the pieces after events like this. Sometimes the families of the perpetrator had it just as awful as the victim's. Either way, they'd still lost someone. Having told the rest of the officers he would meet them at the station, he watched as the cars were driven away, then walked across the yard to Harrison.

Betty looked up as he approached and bleated reproachfully.

"I still don't think she likes me." Blake said as he knelt down.

"She's alright." Harrison said quietly, not looking up. "She's just playful, that's all. Stroke her under the chin and she'll be in love with you."

Blake tickled the goat softly underneath the beard then turned to Harrison. "I know this is a stupid question, but how are you feeling?"

Harrison shook his head. "I don't know. Numb I think."

"Makes sense. It's not easy, what you're going through."

"I just can't believe they did this to me." Harrison murmured. "And what happens now?" He finally looked across at Blake, his face etched into a state of vulnerability and fear. "Are they going to prison?"

Blake nodded. "Yeah." He replied gently.

"How long for?"

"That depends on what the court decides. I couldn't tell you."

"And when would that happen? Would I have to give evidence?"

"I expect so, yeah. Don't worry about that now though. All that matters now is making sure that you're OK. You've had a lot happen to you in a short space of time. If you like, we can arrange counselling, do whatever you need."

"I didn't think I'd ever meet anybody like Dan before we got together. He was so different then, you know. He wasn't anything like what he turned into. He wasn't like my parents."

Blake sighed. He wanted nothing more than to give him a hug. "I know." He shuffled himself down so that he was now sat on the ground next to Harrison, looking across the fields. The sun was starting to set and the only sound that could be heard was the faint clucking of the occasional stray chicken. "Do you have anyone you can stay with?"

Harrison shook his head. "All my friends went to university years ago and I don't really have any close family. It was just me, Mum, Dad and Daniel. I'm going to have to sell this place. I can't afford to live here on my own."

"Don't fancy the life of the lone farmer then?"

Harrison gave him a small smile. "To be honest, I've always hated farming. Getting up at the crack of dawn just to try and keep this place from going bankrupt. It was always my Dad's dream. Personally I'd have been happy just living in a small cottage somewhere. Apart from Betty. I'd take her with me. It sounds stupid but she's been there for me the past few years."

Blake stroked the goat under the chin again as it nuzzled the ground near him. "This will all get easier you know. I know right now it seems like everything's closing in around you, but you'll manage. Considering what you've put up with over these last few years, I think you're probably one of the strongest people I've ever met. It's not the same thing at all, but I know what it's like to lose people that are important to you. Eventually, you do start to move on and live your life again. If you hated it here that much, in some ways this could work out positively for you. You just need to remain strong."

He placed a hand on Harrison's shoulder and gave that tight squeeze again.

Harrison looked up at him. "Thank you." Blake smiled at him and nodded. Someone like Harrison wasn't going to remain single for long. As soon as he put himself out there again, he would be snatched up in a heartbeat. If the circumstances were different and they had met in a bar, Blake himself would probably have been interested. He just hoped that he would be treated better than he had ever been before.

When Blake arrived back at the station, he found Patil, Mattison, Gardiner and Royale waiting for him in the meeting room.

"Ah, Blake." Royale said as he entered. "Good work from everyone today. With the confessions, we should be able to press charges very quickly."

Patil laughed and shook her head in disbelief. "I mean, the *key*. The gun was in the key. I'd never have hit on that."

"We're off to The Dog's Tail, Sir." Mattison said, pulling his coat on. "Are you coming?"

"Blake, can I have a word?" Royale said, standing in the doorway, looking a little stern.

"Yes, Sir?" Blake replied, a little concerned. He turned to Mattison. "I'll meet you there later."

Mattison nodded and he and Patil walked out together. Blake glanced at Gardiner who was sat in the corner, surrounded by paperwork.

"You not going to the pub, Michael?" Blake asked him as he followed Royale into the office.

"No, I'm busy." Replied Gardiner shortly.

Blake shrugged and waited for Royale to close the door behind him.

"Have a seat."

Blake sat and looked up expectantly at Royale.

"Well now." Royale began, sitting down. "We've had you for just a few days and you manage to solve one of the most bizarre murders I think I've ever come across. I have to say, I'm most impressed."

"Thank you, Sir." Smiled Blake.

"However." Royale leant across the desk and looked up at him seriously. "Is it true that you instructed Gardiner to make an arrest, knowing full well that he was putting cuffs on completely the wrong person?"

Blake bit his lip and looked down at the floor. "Erm, yes."

"Well?"

"I knew that the parents were behind it all. And I figured that the quickest way to get to the truth was to…" He paused, circling his hand around to land on how best to explain himself.

Royale got there first. "Was to scare them into thinking they were getting their son sent to prison? Whilst also, I expect, frightening the living daylights out of the lad?"

Blake closed his mouth and grimaced.

"Knowing full well what he'd been through over the past few days, you put that little bit of extra pressure on him to get a quick confession? What if you hadn't been so fortunate? And both the Baxter's had kept quiet? What would you have done with Harrison then?"

Blake sighed. Royale was, of course, completely right. "I was sure that -"

"Not only that," Royale continued sharply. "But you also deceived Gardiner into thinking that his own line of enquiry was completely right." Royale continued. "And made him look and feel like a complete fool."

Blake exhaled. Now it was being put to him like

that, he felt awful. "Yes, Sir."

Royale considered him for a moment, his moustache quivering underneath his nose. "You're clearly an excellent officer, D.S Harte. And will be an incredibly vital component of this station in the months and, I hope, years to come. I am, in no way, taking away what you've achieved with this case. But we're a team here. If you think you've got a culprit then you do *not* keep it to yourself. You do *not* undermine the rest of your colleagues and you do *not* try to act like the hero in an attempt to prove to said colleagues that you were right all along. You also do not under any circumstances repeat today's performances and use false arrests as a means to pressure another suspect. Am I clear?"

Blake felt appropriately admonished. "Yes, Sir. Perfectly. I'm sorry."

"Good." Royale replied. He sighed, then chuckled, shaking his head. "I can certainly see why Gresham found you difficult. Let's try and work together from this point onwards. Now, I've said my piece. Off you go. Enjoy yourself."

"Thank you, Sir." Blake stood up and walked out of the office, closing the door behind him.

An hour later, Blake was stood outside the police station with two pints in his hands. The night had well and truly drawn in by now and the station lights were beaming out of the windows in the silent street around him.

Blake walked inside and through the dark corridors back towards the meeting room. Inside he found who he was looking for. Gardiner was still sat, alone in the room, at the same desk, apparently absorbed in the same paperwork.

Blake walked up to him and placed the pint next to him. Gardiner glanced at it and then up at Blake.

"If Mohammad won't go to the mountain." Blake said to him.

Gardiner put his pen down and looked at the pint. "I said I was busy."

"Well, I've decided, as your superior, that it's time for you to not be busy and relax. This paperwork will still be here tomorrow." Blake replied, leaning against the side of the desk.

There was a pregnant pause.

"And," Blake sighed. "I wanted to apologise to you for how I treated you earlier. I got a proper dressing down by Royale and he was right. I was completely out of order. I'm sorry. It won't happen again."

"Thank you." Gardiner sniffed, picking up his pen and going back to his paperwork again.

"What, is that all I get?"

"What do you want?"

Blake stared at him, annoyed. "I'd like us to be able to move on. We didn't get off to a great start, me and you."

Gardiner merely grunted.

Blake rolled his eyes. "Alright. Have it your way." He stood up and went to walk out the room again. He got to the door and stopped.

"You know, I know that you wanted this job. My job. And I'm sorry if you feel that I've stepped on your toes."

"I have no opinions on your job one way or the other. I do have other things going on in my life." Replied Gardiner brusquely.

Blake walked back into the room again. "I heard things weren't the best for you at home at the moment."

Gardiner's head shot up. "How? What have you heard? Who told you that?" He snapped.

Blake shrugged. "Station gossip. You know what a place of this size can be like."

Gardiner didn't reply.

"Is that why you're here so late?" Blake asked. "Because you don't want to deal with stuff at home?"

"With all due respect, that's absolutely none of your business."

"Yeah, I can't argue with that." Blake conceded. "But you shouldn't bottle it up. I just want to be able to help you, you don't have to deal with it alone. Divorces are crap. They can be absolutely mentally exhausting. Nobody would think any less of you if it was having an effect on you.

Gardiner put down his pen firmly on the desk and glared across the room at Blake. "And what would you know about it? Have you been divorced?"

"Well, not exactly no. But I've recently gone through a pretty nasty breakup. And it hurt. And it made me feel angry at everyone around me who wasn't going through as much crap as me."

Gardiner gave a curt nod. "Run off with another man did she?"

"Not exactly, no."

There was an expectant pause. Blake sighed. It was as good a time as any.

"*He* ran off with a woman."

An expression of shock ran across Gardiner's face. "Oh."

"Yeah." replied Blake. "That was pretty much my reaction."

"Well." Gardiner said, finally taking a sip of the pint Blake had brought him. "That explains a lot."

"Like what?" Blake frowned, sitting down on the desk opposite him.

"Well, it explains why you bit my head off yesterday for what I can only presume you took for homophobia. For what it's worth, it wasn't. I have gay friends."

Blake nodded politely. It didn't seem the time to point out how clichéd that reasoning was.

"So, what about you?" Blake asked. "What's gone on?"

Gardiner sighed. "It turns out that my brother is far too much of a catch for my wife to resist. She told me she was leaving me over dinner one night. Cooked me my favourite, as if that would make it any easier."

This filled Blake with genuine sympathy. "Your brother?"

"My own brother. As it happens, today is also my wedding anniversary. Would have been twenty five years."

Blake exhaled. "Explains why you didn't fancy celebrating in the pub."

"No, I'd rather be here and distract myself from it all. So, there you are. That's my problems. It's been awful, it's been tough and, as you say, mentally exhausting. And I still have a long way to go."

A few moments of silence passed. It felt very strange to Blake that the one person who he apparently had the most common with in this new station was Michael Gardiner.

"I'd better get on with this now." He said, picking up his pen again. "Thanks for the pint."

Blake smiled warmly. "First of many, I hope." He picked up his own glass and they clinked them together.

Gardiner gave him a tight smile back and then carried on writing. Blake stood up, draining the last dregs of beer from his glass. Then, he pulled his ecig out of his pocket and walked out of the room, leaving the man who he now had a newfound respect for alone in the dimly lit meeting room.

UNTOUCHABLE

NINE MONTHS LATER

Sally Ann leant against the pub wall drunkenly, putting her cigarette into her mouth the wrong way.

"I cannot believe that this is your local now." She slurred.

"Why?" Grinned Blake, pulling the cigarette out of her mouth and turning it round. "What's wrong with it?"

"Well, it's just, I mean it's quite quiet round here isn't it?"

"Well it was." Blake replied dryly.

After he had been in Harmschapel for nearly three

quarters of a year, Sally and Blake had finally managed to coincide their time off together so that she could come and visit him. She had arrived that morning and had insisted that he took her round all the local hotspots. She had been quite disappointed when The Dog's Tail had been the only one. She had, however, more than made up for it in terms of how many drinks she had ordered for the pair of them.

"Don't worry, we'll go into town when we've finished these." Blake said, indicating his drink.

"Good." Sally replied, wobbling slightly on her high heels. "It's my mission tonight to find you a man and I don't think we're going to find anybody here. Unless that old bar man takes your fancy."

"Robin? Please, I've not had as many as you. Anyway." Blake laughed. "I don't need a man. I'm perfectly happy."

"Blake?"

Blake turned around to see where the voice had come from. Harrison stood in front of him, a cautious but friendly smile on his face.

"Harrison! How have you been?"

Blake had a fairly good idea how Harrison had been. Over the past few months, anything he hadn't already heard via the station had been told matter-of-factly to him by Robin. Seth and Sandra Baxter had been found guilty of murder and conspiracy to murder respectively and both had received lengthy prison sentences as a result. Blake had only been required to appear in court once during the trial, but the one time he had seen Harrison had almost broken his heart. He had seemed scared, depressed and vulnerable.

Now though, the man in front of him looked quite different. Happy, optimistic and seemed to have a newfound sense of freedom about him.

"I'm doing well." Harrison replied cheerfully. "I've managed to sell the farm. Dad gave me the names for some of his contacts to get a quick and easy sale through. I've managed to find a place to live here in the village. It's got a decent sized garden for Betty."

"Betty?" Blake then laughed. "Oh, you mean the goat."

"And I've got myself a job. Nothing too exciting, just working at Jai Sinnah's shop, but I'm enjoying it."

"Good! I'm so pleased to hear that, I really am." Blake replied.

Harrison grinned. "Thank you."

Sally poked her head over Blake's shoulder. "Hello! I'm Sally. Best friend of this gorgeous man here. And you are?"

"Harrison." He replied, shaking Sally's proffered hand.

"Well, aren't you a stunner?" Sally exclaimed looking him up and down. "Is he one of yours Blake?"

Blake closed his eyes in embarrassment. "Sally-Ann."

"Oh, ignore him." Sally said, waving her hand dismissively. "Harrison. Sorry, hope you don't mind me asking, but are you, well, you know?"

"What?"

"You know. Gay?"

"Sally, for God's sake." Blake said, putting his hands over his face.

Harrison laughed in surprise. "Erm, yeah. Yeah I am."

Sally appeared delighted. "*Are* you? Well, I don't know how well you know Blake, but don't you think he's rather good looking and fabulous?"

Blake groaned in shame. He was going to kill her by the time the night was over. "You don't have to answer that Harrison."

"Yes he does." Sally replied, putting her arm around Blake and waving her hand around as if she was displaying the grand prize on a gameshow. "What do you think Harrison?"

Harrison laughed again, blushing slightly. "Well…Yeah, I do as a matter of fact."

"Excellent!" Sally grinned. "Blake? Don't you think Harrison is a very handsome man?"

Now it was Blake's turn to blush. Sally was getting absolutely no sympathy tomorrow for her inevitable hangover. He looked at Harrison and was mortified to see he seemed to be waiting for an answer. "Alright!" He exclaimed loudly. "Yes, Harrison is very handsome."

"Good." Sally replied. "I'll just leave you two alone." And she tottered back inside the pub, an air of triumph about her.

"I'm so sorry about her." Blake said to Harrison, once she was out of earshot.

"It's alright." Harrison replied, a twinkle in his eye. "I just didn't know you were gay that's all."

Blake fortunately hadn't drank enough to point out that he hadn't mentioned it because he had been investigating the murder of Harrison's ex- boyfriend, so settled for a nonchalant shrug.

Harrison glanced at the pub. "Do you remember the last time me and you were here? I offered to buy you a drink, but you said no, because of the case."

"I do remember that, yes." Smiled Blake.

"Well, can I buy you that drink now?"

Blake chuckled and thought for a moment. "Yeah. Go on then. Seeing as we're practically neighbours now."

Harrison grinned again and walked into the pub. Blake followed him in, a slight spring in his step. As he followed Harrison into the pub, he gave him a firm squeeze on the shoulder. Sometimes, just sometimes, he thought to himself, Sally-Ann really was the best friend in the world.

UNTOUCHABLE

Blake Harte will be back for a brand new mystery **early 2017!**

Printed in Great Britain
by Amazon

25808235R00116